Roddy Doyle

WILDERNESS

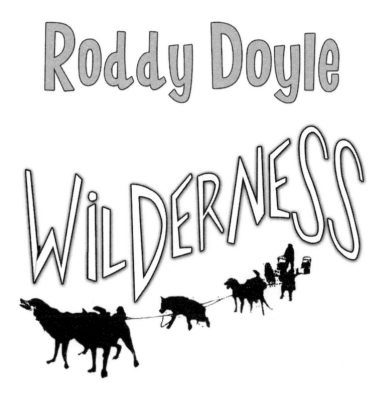

SCHOLASTIC

Dedicated to Liz and Lucy

Scholastic Children's Books
A division of Scholastic Ltd
Euston House, 24 Eversholt Street
London, NW1 1DB, UK
Registered office: Westfield Road, Southam, Warwickshire, CV47 0RA
SCHOLASTIC and associated logos are trademarks and or registered trademarks of
Scholastic Inc.

First published in the US in 2007 by Arthur A. Levine Books,
an imprint of Scholastic Inc.
This edition published in the UK by Scholastic Ltd, 2007

10 digit ISBN 1 407 10231 1 13
digit ISBN 978 1407 10231 3

British Library Cataloguing-in-Publication Data
A CIP catalogue record for this book
is available from the British Library

Printed by Bookmarque Ltd, Croydon, Surrey
Papers used by Scholastic Children's Books are
made from wood grown in sustainable forests.

5 7 9 10 8 6 4

www.scholastic.co.uk/zone

The Eyes

The two boys looked at the dog's eyes.

"What colour are they?" said Johnny.

"Don't know," said Tom.

The eyes were like nothing the boys had ever seen before. There really was no name for their colour.

"Blue?" said Tom.

"No," said Johnny.

"Turquoise?"

"Not really."

The dog stared back at them. Most of the other dogs in the pen were howling and making noises that sounded quite like foreign words. They were rattling and stretching their chains. But this dog in front of them was different. He stood there in the dirty snow, as calm as anything, and looked at the boys, at Tom, and then at Johnny, at Tom, then Johnny.

They weren't really like dog's eyes at all. At least, they weren't like the eyes of any of the dogs the boys knew at home. Lots of their friends had dogs, and their aunt had two of them, but all of those dogs had proper dog eyes. But this dog looking at them had eyes that seemed to belong to a different animal, maybe even a human.

"It's like there's someone trapped in there," said Tom.

Johnny nodded. He knew exactly what his brother meant.

They stepped back, still looking at the dog. They were afraid to turn their backs on him. They stepped back again, into thick, clean snow. They did it again, and bumped into something hard. They turned, and looked up at the biggest, tallest, widest man they'd ever seen.

The man was a solid wall in front of them. The dog was right behind them.

"Why – are – you – here?" said the man.

CHAPTER ONE

Johnny Griffin was nearly twelve and his brother, Tom, was ten. They lived in Dublin, with their parents and their sister. They were two ordinary boys. And they were being very ordinary the day their mother made the announcement.

They were in the kitchen, doing their homework. It was raining outside, and the rain was hammering on the flat roof of the kitchen. So they didn't hear their mother's key in the front door and they didn't hear her walking up the hall. Suddenly, she was there.

They always loved it when she came home from work, but this was even better, because she was soaking wet. There was already a pool at her feet.

"I'm a bit wet, lads," she said.

She shook herself, and big drops of secondhand rain flew at the boys and made them shout and laugh. She grabbed them and pressed their faces into her soggy jacket. Tom laughed again, but Johnny didn't. He thought he was too old for this.

"Let go!" he yelled into the jacket.

"Say please," said his mother.

"No!" said Johnny.

But she let him go, and his brother too.

"There'll be no rain where we're going, lads," she said.

That sounded interesting.

"Only snow."

That sounded very interesting.

So she told them what she'd done that day, at lunchtime. She'd been walking past a travel shop and something bright in the window caught her eye. She stopped and looked. It was a hill in the window, made of artificial snow, and there was a teddy bear skiing down the hill. It was an ad for winter holidays.

"It was really stupid, lads," she said. "The poor teddy was wearing a crash helmet that was way too big for him and his skis were on back to front. But, sure anyway, I went in and booked a holiday for us."

"Where?" said Johnny.

"Finland."

The boys went mad. Tom ran down the hall, up the stairs, jumped on the beds and came back.

"Where's Finland?" he asked.

They got Johnny's atlas out of his schoolbag and

found Finland. Their mother showed them the route they'd be taking. Her finger went from Dublin, over the Irish Sea.

"We've to fly to Manchester first," she said.

And her finger turned at Manchester, and headed north across the page.

"And then to Helsinki."

They liked the sound of that place.

"Helsinki! Helsinki!"

They thumped each other and laughed.

"And then," said their mother, "we change planes again and fly even further north."

Her finger went up from Helsinki, and stopped.

"To a place that isn't on the map," she said.

"Why not?" said Tom.

"It's probably too small," said Johnny.

"That's right," said their mother.

"What's it called?"

"I can't remember," said their mother. "And I left the brochure at work. But it looks lovely."

"When are we going?" said Johnny.

"In two weeks," she said.

"Deadly," said Tom.

"But we'll still be in school," said Johnny.

He'd worked it out. It was the middle of November. Add two weeks and they'd be at the beginning of December, still three weeks before the Christmas holidays.

"No, you won't," said their mother. "I already phoned Ms Ford."

Ms Ford was the principal of their school. Johnny was in sixth class, and Tom was in fifth.

"She said she was inclined to look favourably at my request, because it'll be such an educational experience for both of you."

"Does that mean we can go?" said Johnny.

"Yes," said their mother. "She said fire away, but to be sure to bring her home a present."

So that was it. They were going to Finland.

"Coo-il!"

That much was true. But some of the things their mother had told Johnny and Tom weren't true at all. She'd told them she'd left the brochure on her desk at work. But she hadn't. It was in her bag. But she didn't want them running off and rooting through her bag. There were things in there that she didn't want the boys to see. She'd told them that the teddy in the window was wearing a helmet that was too big, and skis that were back to front. That wasn't true. Because there was no teddy. And she'd told them she'd gone straight in and booked the holiday. But that wasn't true either. She *had* booked the holiday at lunchtime that day. But she'd been thinking about doing it for weeks.

Johnny and Tom's mother was called Sandra. Sandra Hammond.

"Is Dad going with us?" Tom asked later, when they were having their dinner.

Their father's name was Frank. Frank Griffin.

"No," said Sandra.

"Why not?"

"Well," said Sandra. "It's an adventure holiday. And you know your dad. His idea of an adventure is going to the front door to get the milk."

"What about Gráinne?"

Gráinne was their sister.

"No," said Sandra. "She won't be coming either."

"How come?" said Johnny.

"She wouldn't want to," said Sandra.

Tom and Johnny didn't mind. Their mother was right. Gráinne wouldn't want to go with them, even to as cool a place as Finland. Gráinne was much older than the boys. She was eighteen. And Tom and Johnny didn't like her much. Mainly because she didn't like them.

Their father came home. They heard the music. He always played it loud, with the car windows down, but only when he turned into the drive. He did it to annoy their neighbour. It was a long story. Or, at least, it went back a long time. It went way back, to when Gráinne was only three, and Frank was married to a woman called Rosemary, and they were moving into the house. Frank was helping the removal men carry a couch into the house. But he wasn't being much help.

Actually, he was in the way. He was standing at the door watching Gráinne. She was talking to a woman who was cutting her side of the hedge. This was Mrs Newman, their new neighbour, although she wasn't new at all – she was at least forty. And Gráinne was talking to her.

"Hello," she said.

But the new neighbour wasn't talking back.

"Hello, lady," said Gráinne.

Mrs Newman just kept chopping the hedge.

"Hello, lady," said Gráinne.

Frank hopped over the couch and went straight over to the hedge.

"My daughter has been saying hello to you," he said.

"What?" said Mrs Newman.

"She's been saying hello to you," said Frank.

"I didn't hear her," said Mrs Newman.

She didn't really look at Frank. She leaned out and chopped a bit of hedge with the shears. It fell at Frank's feet.

"I'm a bit deaf," she said.

"Oh," said Frank.

He put his hand out, over the hedge.

"I'm Frank Griffin, by the way."

But Mrs Newman didn't shake Frank's hand. In fact, she nearly chopped his fingers off. He took his hand back just in time. He felt the breeze on his fingertips as the two blades snapped together.

He picked up Gráinne and carried her into their new house. He didn't speak to Mrs Newman again, but he didn't start playing the music loud until much later, about three years after they'd moved into the house. It was the sad part of the story. Frank and Rosemary weren't happily married any more. He didn't know why not, and neither did she. It just seemed to happen. They didn't love each other any more. And they argued. About small things, about stupid things. They had a big argument about a rotten apple Frank found in the bottom of Gráinne's schoolbag. The apple mush had seeped into two of her copy books, and he blamed Rosemary for it. He knew he was being mean. But he couldn't help himself. That was what it felt like – he wanted to stop but he couldn't.

"If you had any interest in her education you'd have found that apple before it exploded in her bag," he said.

He was shouting.

"And what about you?" said Rosemary.

She was shouting back. They were in their bedroom, at the front of the house. It was a nice night, in September. The window was wide open. Frank saw it, the open window, and he didn't care.

"Where's *your* interest in her education?" said Rosemary.

"I'm more interested than you," said Frank. "That's for sure."

The argument went on like that. It was really stupid and pointless.

The doorbell rang. Rosemary looked out the window and saw the police car.

"Oh, God," she said.

They both went down to answer the door. The two Guards, a man and a woman, looked embarrassed and very young. There'd been a complaint about noise, they told Frank. The woman, the Bean Garda, did the talking. Rosemary was right behind Frank, looking at the Guards over his shoulder. Frank apologized, and Rosemary behind him nodded too. They were both very sorry.

"Yes, well," said the Bean Garda.

She was looking carefully at both of them, Frank suddenly realized, and he wanted the floor to open up and swallow him. She was looking for bruises, or red skin, proof that they'd been violent.

"It was just a row," said Frank. "Sorry."

The Bean Garda had finished her examination.

"Well," she said. "We all have them now and again. But maybe you could close the windows the next time, Mr Griffin."

Frank laughed but, really, he'd never felt less like laughing in his life. He felt so humiliated and awful – he just wanted to shut the door. And that was what he was doing when he saw the cigarette. They both saw it. It was dark out there, especially when the police car turned and went. But there it was, the glowing cigarette, at the other side of the hedge. Mrs Newman was behind the cigarette, looking at them. And they knew. She was the one who'd phoned the Guards.

"She's only deaf when it suits her," said Frank as he shut the door.

Frank and Rosemary hugged each other in the hall. They went into the kitchen, made tea, and agreed that they couldn't live together any more. It was a terrible night, and Frank always blamed Mrs Newman for it. He knew he wasn't being fair. But when he thought about that night, and the days and months that led up to it, he always saw that glowing cigarette. Thirteen years after that night, eight years after Mrs Newman gave up smoking, Frank still played loud music when he drove into the drive, just to let her know. He *knew* – she wasn't deaf at all. He wasn't angry any more. But he still liked to annoy Mrs Newman.

Johnny and Tom met him at the front door.

"We're going to Finland," said Tom.

"Make sure you're home in time for bed," said Frank.

"In two weeks," said Tom.

"Are you serious?" said Frank.

He took his jacket off and hung it on the bannister.

"Yeah," said Johnny. "We're going with Mam."

"Come down to the kitchen and tell me all about it," said Frank.

But he knew all about it already. It had actually been his idea. And the excitement on the boys' faces was the best thing he'd seen in a long time.

The day after their last argument, Rosemary made Gráinne's lunch for school. She helped Gráinne put on her coat, and then she walked with Gráinne down the road to the school. She kissed Gráinne, and hugged her.

"Bye-bye, honey-boo," she said. "Have a lovely day."

Then she stood at the school railings and watched Gráinne as she walked across the yard and in the door. She was crying and she didn't care that people were looking at her. She walked home and packed two suitcases. Gráinne's granny collected Gráinne from school, and Frank collected her from her granny's house on his way home from work. Rosemary was gone when Frank and Gráinne got home.

"Where's Mama?" said Gráinne.

"She's gone on a holiday," said Frank.

That was the question, and that was the answer for days after that, and then another question was added.

"When's she coming home?"

And another answer.

"In a while."

And another question.

"When?"

And the answer.

"I don't know."

Then Gráinne stopped asking the questions.

For a long time Frank heard nothing about Rosemary. He found out that she'd gone to America. Then he heard she was living in New York. She phoned her parents a few times a year, and sent her love to Gráinne. But that was all.

For a long while, it was just him and Gráinne. And it was fine. They were lonely, but they were lonely together. Gráinne missed her mother, and stopped believing that she'd ever come home. But she loved her father and he was always there, smiling, always downstairs when she was falling asleep, always awake before her. Always her father.

Then he met Sandra.

They met at a concert. She was there with her boyfriend, and she was sitting in Frank's seat.

He looked again at his ticket.

"M17," he said. "You're in my seat, sorry."

"Really?" she said.

Her boyfriend, on the other side, stood up.

"What's the story?" he said.

"It's my seat," said Frank.

The boyfriend looked at Frank's ticket. Then he looked at his own.

"N18," he said. "We're in the wrong row. Oops."

He left his seat, and Frank sat down beside Sandra. And, by the end of the concert, they were in love, even though Sandra's boyfriend was sitting right behind them. She explained it to Frank, later.

"It was the way you listened," she said. "You leaned forward in your seat. You really listened. I loved that. And you have a lovely nose. What was it about me?"

"Everything," said Frank.

He meant it. He loved everything about Sandra. He even loved the way she'd coughed when she swallowed a sweet during one of the quiet songs.

"What about Jason?" said Frank.

Jason was the old boyfriend.

"Ah well," said Sandra. "He was all right. But I could never really love a man who says oops."

Sandra met Gráinne, and they liked each other. Gráinne was six. Sandra made her laugh a lot, and Gráinne thought she was beautiful, and she liked the way her dad looked at her. He laughed a lot too.

And three weeks after that, Frank took Gráinne to the Bad Ass Café, just the two of them, and he told her that Sandra was going to move into the house with them, and how did she feel about that?

"What about Mammy?" she said.

"She lives in New York," said Frank. "She probably needed to get away. For a while, maybe. She loves you, Gráinne, but not me. You can go to New York to see her. When you're a bit older."

So Gráinne nodded and said, "Fine." She liked Sandra. It would be nice.

And it was. Sandra wasn't much good at cooking but she was funny and lovely, and she sang a lot. They went shopping together, and she bought Gráinne clothes that Frank never thought of – jeans and tops, socks and knickers. Frank always bought her party dresses and skirts, and coloury tights and necklaces. They went driving a lot, the three of them, up the mountains and to Howth or Malahide.

Then one morning, Gráinne woke up. It was still dark outside, so she went into Frank's room, to get into the bed beside Frank. And Sandra was in the bed beside Frank, both of them asleep. Gráinne stood looking at them. She was cold. She got into the bed, beside Frank. He hugged her. His eyes were still closed. He turned, still hugging her, and she was between them, squashed between Frank and Sandra, and it was fine. It was lovely and warm. When she woke up again it was bright outside, and the bed was empty, and she heard laughter from downstairs. Frank and Sandra were laughing.

Then, another day, months later, they took her to the Bad Ass again and they told her – Sandra told her. She was pregnant, she was going to have a baby.

"Are you the daddy?" she asked Frank.

Frank was shocked at the question, and impressed. Gráinne was looking straight at him.

"Yes," said Frank. "The baby will be your sister or brother."

"No, it won't," said Gráinne.

She worked it out.

"It'll only be my *half*-sister, or half-brother."

"But it's great news, isn't it?" said Sandra.

"Yeah," said Gráinne.

But, really, she didn't know what it was, good or bad, or even news at all. She didn't know what she felt.

The baby was Johnny. And Gráinne loved him, he was so cute. Sandra was at home all the time now and, even though she was often busy feeding Johnny and playing with Johnny, Gráinne loved it. She was old enough to walk home from school on her own, and Sandra was always there when Gráinne rang the bell or went around to the back door and, nearly always, her dinner was ready, the smell of it filling the kitchen. She sometimes felt alone, and a few times, when she went into her dad's room to get into the bed, he asked her to go back to her own bed because Johnny was already in the middle and there was no more room.

"He's a brute," said Frank. "Look at the size of him."

But Frank and Sandra made sure Gráinne wasn't left alone for long. She loved it when Frank got down on the floor beside her and played. He did it a lot, and so did Sandra. Gráinne knew that they were looking after her. They checked her homework, checked that her clothes were clean, checked her hair for head lice when the letter came from school.

"Uh-oh, the lice letter."

"It's the same one every time," said Gráinne. "The exact same words."

"That's not fair on the lice," said Sandra. "Every louse is different. Come here, till we look."

Then they took Gráinne to the Bad Ass again, and Tom was born soon after. He was cute too, but Sandra was mad busy, and Johnny was very jealous. He climbed and pushed his way on to Sandra's lap when she was feeding Tom. He threw his food across the kitchen. He dumped it on top of his head. He did anything to get Sandra to look at him. There wasn't much room for Gráinne. But Frank always kissed and hugged her first when he came home, even though, sometimes, Johnny bit his leg while he was hugging her. And he often took her out for special times together. They even went to Paris for a long weekend. It was OK, living in that house, growing up with Frank and Sandra, and Johnny and Tom. Gráinne was happy.

Then she was a teenager and suddenly, it seemed, she was unhappy and unfriendly, and silent and loud at the same time. She spoke to no one, but slammed the doors. She turned her music up loud, talked loudly to her friends on her mobile phone, telling them how stupid her family was and how she hated them all. It was teenage stuff, Frank and Sandra knew, but it was hard. Especially for Frank. He felt guilty and, sometimes, angry. She was like this because he was a bad father – there was something he wasn't doing right. Other times, he decided she was just a selfish wagon, like her mother, and the sooner she grew up and got out of the house the better. And then he'd feel guilty again. He was the selfish one. She was a teenager; it was a phase she was going through. It would end and they'd be pals again.

"Fancy going to the Bad Ass?" he said one Friday, when he came home and she was by herself in the hall.

"No," she said.

"Just the two of us," said Frank.

"Like, wow," she said, and she went up the stairs. He felt her door slamming. The whole house shook a bit.

"You're not my mother!" she roared at Sandra. More and more often.

It was rough.

"It'll only last a few years," Sandra told Frank, even though she'd just been crying because of something Gráinne had said to her. "I was like that myself when I was her age."

"Yeah," said Frank.

But he didn't sound convinced.

He stayed out of Gráinne's way. He didn't interfere, and he hoped she was doing OK at school. He hoped she wasn't being stupid when she went out at night, on the weekends. He always stayed awake until she came home, but always in bed. He didn't want her to think that he was spying on her. The next day, he always asked her how she'd got on, and he never looked too closely at her eyes or tried to smell her breath. He kept his distance and respected her independence. But it was hard.

She was caught mitching from school, and suspended for two weeks. She was caught shoplifting. Mrs Fallon, from the shop at the end of the road, didn't phone the Guards, but it was awful. Frank apologized, and thanked her, and bought loads of things he didn't need or want.

Gráinne left school two months before the Leaving Cert exams. She wouldn't go back.

"You can't make me," she said.

And that was the really terrifying bit: she was right. They couldn't make her. They just had to hope she'd be OK, that she'd calm down and become Gráinne again, their Gráinne.

But, for now, she was a different Gráinne. A monster, a big, horrible kid. A terrorist. It was after she threw the cup at Sandra that Frank suggested that Sandra and the boys needed a break.

He wrapped the broken pieces in some newspaper.

They could get away for a while, he said. It would be good for them. It might even be good for Frank and Gráinne to have the house to themselves. Like the old days.

"Like the *good* old days," said Sandra. "Before I arrived."

"Ah stop," said Frank.

"No," she said. "I won't."

She was still shaking. The cup had just missed her head. She looked at the coffee stains on the wall and on her blouse. She took off the blouse and soaked it in cold water. Frank put the newspaper into the bin and wiped the wall.

"I'm not going anywhere," said Sandra. "And what about the money?"

"We'll manage," said Frank. "We can do without a holiday in the summer."

"No," said Sandra, finally. "She's not going to push me out of my own home. It *is* my home."

"I'll talk to her" said Frank.

"Give me a break," said Sandra. "Just shoot her."

It was quiet enough for a few months. It wasn't too bad. They all kept out of Gráinne's way, and she kept out of theirs. The days got colder and shorter. Sandra came home one day and found the three of them, Johnny, Tom, and Gráinne, watching the telly. They were all on the couch, long legs and arms all over the place. It was the sweetest thing she'd seen in a long time. But Gráinne saw her looking at them. She took back her arms and legs, stood up, and walked out of the room, past Sandra. Black eyes, black lips in a sneer that would have been funny on someone else's daughter – stepdaughter.

Then the news came. Gráinne's mother, Rosemary, was coming home.

"Oh, God," said Sandra. "How do you know?"

"Her mother phoned me," said Frank.

"I don't want to meet her," said Sandra.

"Fine," said Frank. "We can work that out. No problem."

"For good?" said Sandra.

"What?" said Frank.

"Stop being thick, Frank," said Sandra. "Is she coming home for good?"

"Oh," said Frank. "I don't know. Her mother didn't seem to know."

Sandra stood up, and sat down, and stood up. Frank tried to hug her, but she sat down again as his arms went out to her.

"I've changed my mind," she said. "I'm going away. Me and the boys. I can't stay here."

And the day after that, she came home in the rain and told the boys the good news.

The Bedroom

She sat on her bed. Her eyes were closed. Her arms were wrapped around her knees. Her knees were right up to her chin.

She could hear them. Talking about her.

She couldn't. Her music was all she could hear. But she *knew* what they were saying about her. Down in the kitchen. She could hear them. They hated her.

They hated her. And she hated them.

CHAPTER TWO

There were things they had to get. Thermal underwear – long-sleeved vests and long underpants down to their ankles – gloves, special socks, hats, scarves.

"What about skis?" said Tom.

"No," said Sandra.

"What about a canoe?"

"Nope."

The shop was full of outdoor adventure stuff. Canoes hanging from the roof, and tents all over the place. But all they were buying was socks and gloves. Johnny picked up a mountaineering hammer.

"What about one of these?"

"Each," said Tom.

"No," said Sandra. "Put it back."

"We might need them."

"Put – it – back."

"We might."

"Put. It. Back."

Johnny and Tom had been outside the back door when they heard the cup hitting the wall. Johnny had his hand on the door handle. They stayed there. They were both a bit scared. Johnny waited to hear more from inside, but there was nothing. He looked at Tom.

"OK?"

"OK."

They went in, Johnny went first. Their mother was at the sink, in her black bra, the one that used to be new. They noticed that the wall beside her was wet and very clean.

"I spilt bloody coffee on myself," she said.

"Oh," said Johnny. "Can we watch telly?"

They weren't allowed to watch telly on school days.

"OK," said their mother.

And they knew for definite that something was wrong, and they went in and watched *Complete Savages*.

"My mother's going to take me away from this dump," Gráinne told them.

"Cool," said Tom. "I'll get your room."

"No, you won't!" Gráinne roared, and she slammed the door.

"What's her mother called?" Tom asked Johnny.

"Rosemary," said Johnny.

"Do you think she'll really take her away?"

"Hope so," said Johnny.

They knew that things weren't completely OK. But, as far as they knew, they were going on their holidays to Lapland, in northern Finland, and that was all. They were going to a place with snow and reindeer and huskies and snowmobiles.

Their dad drove them to the airport, and it was typical early-morning adult talk, all the way.

"Will you have to wait long in Manchester?"

"No."

"Grand."

"An hour, I think."

"That's not too bad."

"No, it's fine."

He didn't come into the airport with them; he had to get to work. But he got out of the car and hugged them. It was kind of sad that he wasn't coming, but Tom was happy they were going with just their mother. It was special, and she was always a bit crazier when their dad wasn't around. She'd let them run up the down escalator if it wasn't too crowded, and push each other on trolleys. But not this time; they had to go straight to the departure gate after they'd checked in. And then they were in the plane and in the air, and down again, in Manchester Airport, and straight to the next plane and in the air again. Nothing happened, except Johnny had to open his bag for a security man who searched inside and found no guns or weapons.

They had to wait for an hour and a half in Helsinki Airport, for the plane to Lapland, and Sandra went to the toilet three times.

"For a smoke," said Tom, as they watched her cross the wide corridor.

"Yeah," said Johnny.

"What's in the women's toilets that isn't in the men's?"

"Don't know. What?"

"Women."

"Thick."

"Muppet."

"Thick."

Then they were up again, their third flight in one day. Johnny had the window seat.

"It's not fair," said Tom.

"I'm the oldest," said Johnny.

"So?"

"Shut up."

"Now, now, lads," said Sandra. "You can swap halfway."

But they didn't, because the plane began its descent while they were still arguing – they were less than half an hour in the air. They could see big snow at the side of the runway. And the snow, small mountains of it, the deep tyre tracks, the whiteness, and the airport lights made them forget about the row and everything else. There was only the next six days.

There was a man standing at the arrivals gate with a sign, WINTER SAFARIS, held to his chest. Sandra and the boys walked up to him.

"Winter safaris?" said Sandra.

"Winter safaris," said the man. "Yes. Come, please."

They followed the man through the tiny airport to a minibus. It was right outside the exit. He opened the rear door, and took their bags, and shoved them in with other bags. Then he opened the side door and stood back. They got in, and there were three other people in there, at the back. Sandra, Tom and Johnny squeezed into the seat right behind the driver's seat, and the driver slid the side door behind them, and disappeared.

They sat there for half an hour, watching their breath and saying very little.

"Cold?"

"Yeah; no."

Tom looked back at the three people behind them. The one in the middle was asleep, and the other two were whispering to each other, across the sleeping woman's face. They were a boy and a girl, in big padded clothes and hats. They leaned over the sleeping face and kissed, and Tom stopped looking.

They heard the rear door being opened, a grunt, and the door slammed shut. Then there was a blast of very cold air. The driver's door was open and he was getting in.

He looked over his seat at them.

"Apology for lateness. I must see a man about a dog."

And then they heard it.

A bark.

There was a dog in the back. They looked. The woman still slept; the other two whispered. Johnny couldn't see the dog. But it barked again, and let out a howl. And barked again, and stopped when the driver started the minibus.

"Welcome to Lapland," he said.

"Thank you," said Sandra.

"You are welcome."

"How long is it to the camp?"

The driver shrugged, and took a big right turn that sent the boys pushing into Sandra, and they kept pushing long after the driver had straightened up, Johnny into Tom, both of them into Sandra, until she told them to stop. They were excited again now that they were moving, and they could see lines of trees made fat with snow – joined by snow, as if the trees were holding hands – and house lights shining across fields of snow that hadn't been touched yet.

They drove slowly through a town the driver told them was called Muonio. They passed a long, flat building.

"Last school before the Arctic Circle," he said.

And another.

"Last hospital. . . Last supermarket."

He turned right and stopped in front of a row of wooden houses, and got out. The door behind them slid open and the cold slid in, and the woman who'd been sleeping smiled before she stepped out. Johnny heard her chatting to the driver. They laughed, and he heard the rear door – the boot – open and close, and the driver got back in and started the minibus.

"Soon," he said.

Another left, a right, and the driver stopped again, in front of a two-storey building. This time, he didn't get out. The boy and girl picked up rucksacks and shopping bags. They pushed on the side door. Again, the cold came in. The boy and girl climbed out. They heard the boot being opened.

"Students," said the driver.

He nodded at the building.

"College. They learn to be guides."

He nodded to the back of the bus.

"Not very good, I think. They cannot find skis."

He got out of the bus and grunted his way past their window to the back. They heard scraping and banging – no barking – and the boot was slammed again. The driver came back the other way, so he could shut the sliding door.

"Very soon," he said as he climbed back in. "Long day."

"Yes," said Sandra.

They were off again, slowly, to the end of the street

where there was just darkness ahead of them. He did a slow U-turn, and they went back past the little college and the two students struggling towards it, covered in bags and skis. A few more turns, and the town was behind them. They were on a straight road, streetlights for a while, then gone. And trees, in lines beside them, pushed low by the weight of the snow, branches out, holding hands, keeping the minibus safe on the road.

The trees were gone now on the right side, and they saw a long black gap that the driver told them was the river.

"Sweden," he said. "Other side."

They passed a bridge and, halfway across it, the border checkpoint. The lights were out, the roadblocks down.

"Can we go across to Sweden one of the days?" said Tom.

"Yes," said Sandra. "Why not?"

"Cool."

"Sweden."

"Two countries."

"Three," said Johnny. "England as well. Manchester Airport, remember?"

"Oh, yeah. Cool."

The driver slowed down, as if he was searching for something in the trees, and then he turned right, and they saw that they were on a road that had been well hidden. The trees on the left weren't there any more and the hotel was. They liked it immediately. Johnny smiled at Tom, and Tom smiled back.

"Coo-il."

It was a low, long wooden building that seemed to be hiding in the snow. It was surrounded by smaller buildings, some lit, some dark, all like something built for a film. The minibus swung into a wide space – a car park, maybe, but no cars. There were banks of thick snow on each side of the hotel door, and untouched snow all around them, lit by high lights that made it brighter than any snow they'd seen before.

By the time the driver pulled open the side door, Johnny and Tom were shoving each other to be first at the snow. Sandra heard, then felt, the crunch of the snow under her boots. It wasn't as cold as she'd expected. It wasn't really cold at all. She followed the boys to the back of the minibus. The driver opened the door, and stepped back to lift it. And they stepped back to avoid him. They moved from behind his back and looked – no dog. He pulled out their bags. Still no dog. He put the boys' bags on the ground.

"Hey, mister," said Johnny. "Where's the dog?"

"Dog?"

"The dog you put in at the airport."

"Got out in town," said the driver. "Met a lady dog."

He laughed, and handed Sandra her bag, and, she thought, he winked.

"Come on, lads," she said.

The boys were up to their knees in snow, wondering where to start.

"Later," said Sandra. "Let's see what the room's like."

"Ah."

They went inside, to the reception desk.

"Coo-il," said Tom.

There were knives for sale, in a glass cabinet behind the counter. Their granddad used to show them the blades on his Swiss army knife when they went to his house on Sundays. But these knives were different. They were shining steel, nothing hiding the blades – they were dangerous even to look at.

"Can we've a knife?"

"Each?"

"No."

Sandra was filling in a form for the woman behind the counter.

"We'll pay with our own money," said Johnny.

"No."

They tried to see the prices on the knives. There were little tags attached to the handles with pieces of string. They leaned across the counter, but Johnny could get further because he was taller than Tom, and his body and jacket pushed Tom back. And, suddenly, Tom was angry. Tom was growing too, but he could never catch up with Johnny, and this always happened – he ended up in second place, in the back seat, with the smaller potato, the broken toy. He could feel tears climbing to the eyes, and that wasn't fair either, because Johnny would start laughing at him.

He hit Johnny. He slapped his back. His hand bounced off Johnny's jacket; it couldn't have hurt him. But the noise was like an explosion, and it made Sandra jump. The pen she was holding skipped across the paper. She had to get between Johnny and Tom before the fight got going.

"Stop that! Now!"

She was embarrassed, and that made her angry – because she hated being embarrassed, and she hated herself for being embarrassed.

"Do you want to get us thrown out?" she said. "Before we even get in? Well?"

"No," said Tom.

"Well?"

"No," said Johnny.

"So, stop."

"Sorry."

"Yes, well."

She got the key to their room and led the way. The floor was stone; the doors they passed were big and wooden. The corridor was nicely dark. There were lights, but they couldn't see them. Sandra stopped at a door, and they saw now that the key was huge, like a key from a film with pirates or prisons in it. She unlocked the door, and then a strange thing – the door opened outwards. They had to step back, and then go into the room.

"Wow!" said Sandra.

She loved the room. It was huge, and almost dark. The main bed was as wide as a field. And the bunk beds were even bigger. There was space for the boys and every friend they'd ever had. The whole place was wood, just nicely warm and—

"Hey!"

Johnny found it, beside the toilet. A sauna.

"God," said Sandra.

She sat on the bed, and lay back – the most comfortable, warmest, coolest bed she'd ever been on. She closed her eyes. This was all she'd wanted.

"Want to go out and play, lads?"

They were already getting into their blue thermal underwear, the leggings and the long-sleeved vests. They were dressed again, and gone.

"Seeyeh," said Johnny.

Sandra sat up, got her boots off, and lay back on the bed.

The boys legged it down the corridor, past the reception and the knives – the woman behind the counter smiled – out the front door, and into the darkness and snow. Johnny grabbed a handful and made a ball. Tom did the same. They faced each other, laughed, and got ready to throw.

Then they heard the howl.

The Bus

Gráinne was on the bus to the airport. Alone. The way she wanted it. She was meeting her mother. By herself.

She looked out the window. It was still dark, and cold.

The bus was on the motorway now. They'd be there soon.

She took out the photograph. The speed of the bus made her hand shake. She put it back in her bag. She'd know her without the photograph. She'd know.

CHAPTER THREE

It wasn't just one dog. They realized that as they walked across the wide space in front of the hotel. There were two dogs, two different howls. The snow here was ice, packed solid by heavy boots. They slid a bit, and Tom fell. He wasn't hurt. He laughed, and Johnny helped him up. They moved towards a high wire fence. There were lights here too, much higher than the streetlights in Dublin. But it was darker than the front of the hotel. They were moving nearer the trees too, and they could hear the wind in the branches, and the lights swayed. The wind made a singing, screeching noise and in it Johnny heard the howls of the dogs. And he knew: There were more than two dogs – lots more.

They reached the fence. It was way up over them, like a fence around a prison. They were really cold for the first time. The snow had seeped through their gloves. They were nearer the howls now. "It's just dog noise," said Tom.

"Yeah," said Johnny.

They kept going.

Johnny saw the lane beside the fence, to their right. He pointed, and walked that way. He walked differently on the ice. He had to lift his legs higher than usual, and put each foot down flat on the ground. And he held his arms out from his sides. It was either that or slide.

They got to the entrance of the lane and saw that it widened ahead of them. A high branch swayed and blocked the nearest light. They were right under the trees; they formed one side of the lane. Tom could hear them groan, and something, a branch, some ice, snapped not far away. Tom moved closer to his brother.

They stopped. It was really, really cold.

"Look."

A line of them.

"Snowmobiles."

Parked side by side, about ten of them.

"Coo-il."

Tom wasn't frightened now; he hadn't really been frightened anyway. There were people around somewhere, people who parked their snowmobiles.

They walked towards the snowmobiles. And now, ahead of them a good bit, they saw small, stomach-high sheds that they both guessed were kennels. It was like a village of kennels. The kennels were great, real doghouses. They couldn't see the dogs yet. But Johnny could smell them.

"God."

Tom laughed.

"Dog breath," he said.

Then he heard a howl that didn't sound funny. He kept going, close to Johnny, over the icy ground, nearer to the kennels, and the first dog he noticed was standing on the roof of his kennel. Staring at Tom. And there was another, in front of his kennel, eating from a bowl. And another beside him, drinking water. All staring at Tom.

The wind was blowing straight at Johnny. It was cold and almost solid; it made his eyes dry. The dogs were silent now, but they were looking straight at him and Tom, even the ones that were eating. He could hear their teeth.

"They're not that big," said Tom, quietly – Johnny could hardly hear him.

"Look," said Johnny. "They're chained."

The chains were long and fixed to the sides of the kennels. One of the dogs howled, and others all around joined in. It was a noise Johnny didn't hear that much from dogs at home, but it wasn't that fierce or frightening. The huskies were chained but they were wagging their tails, and yapping. They really weren't as big as Johnny had expected, and they didn't look too wild. Two or three of them stretched their chains to get to Johnny and Tom, but they didn't lunge at them or growl. None of them barked. They were curious. And the smell made the boys laugh.

Tom had never seen so much poo. It was all over the place, sitting on the snow, lodged in the ice, steaming new, and ancient. He walked carefully. He was in among the dogs. He could see the breath, and feel the heat on his cheeks, even though he didn't bend or go too near.

"Look at their eyes," said Johnny.

Tom was already looking at them. They all had the most amazing eyes. One of them, pure white, had a different colour for each eye, a brown one and a blue. And one of them, Johnny saw, had different colours in one eye. He was going to show it to Tom, when they were suddenly in front of one dog that made them stop.

It wasn't that the dog snarled, or even growled. It was nothing like that. He stepped away from his kennel, and kind of turned, just a bit, to face them. And he stood there, still, in front of them. They knew: he was blocking their way. A leader. Maybe *the* leader. They knew, and they didn't have to say it.

They didn't move. They stayed still and looked at the dog's eyes.

"What colour are they?" said Johnny.

"Don't know," said Tom.

The eyes were like nothing the boys had ever seen before. There really was no name for their colour.

"Blue?" said Tom.

"No," said Johnny.

"Turquoise?"

"Not really."

The dog stared back at them. He stood there in the dirty snow, as calm as anything, and looked at the boys, at Tom, and then at Johnny, at Tom, then Johnny.

They weren't really like a dog's eyes at all.

"It's like there's someone trapped in there," said Tom.

Johnny nodded. He knew exactly what Tom meant.

They stepped back, still looking at the dog. They were afraid to turn their backs on him. They stepped back again, into thick, clean snow. They did it again, and bumped into something hard. They turned, and looked up at the biggest, tallest, widest man they'd ever seen.

The man was a solid wall in front of them. The dog was right behind them.

"Why – are – you – here?" said the man.

Tom had to look up, and up, to see him properly. He had to stretch his neck right back. He hoped he'd see a smile when he got to the man's face. But there was no smile.

"You – should – not – be – here," said the man.

"Sorry," said Tom.

The dogs around them were pulling their chains

and whimpering. The man said something in Finnish to the dogs. They were pulling at their chains, trying to drag their doghouses to the man. They liked him. Johnny could see that, and so could Tom.

But that didn't make him a nice man. A murderer could be nice to his dog. The man stood huge in front of them, right over them. He had a knife on his belt, like one of the ones they'd seen in the hotel, but longer. They both saw it at the same time. It was hanging there, in front of their eyes. It was old and used-looking; the blade was scratched. The wood of the handle was black from years of sweat and maybe blood.

Johnny felt something behind his knee.

The dog.

His left knee. The dog poked it, with his nose. Like he wanted to topple him.

Johnny didn't look.

He heard the dog sniff. He felt its breath through his trousers – he thought he did.

"Come," said the man.

They got out of his way. It wasn't easy – the ice and poo. He walked between Johnny and Tom. And he walked through the dogs, past the kennels. He wasn't wearing a hat or cap. The dogs pulled at their chains. They whimpered.

The boys looked at each other and followed the man, to a wall behind the kennels. There were bales of straw, covered by a big sheet of blue plastic. The man pulled back the plastic. It exploded in the wind – that was what it sounded like. It lifted, and flapped, and tried to fly away. He shook it and threw it on to the dirty snow. He kicked a rock on to it. It still lifted and dropped, but couldn't escape. The boys stayed well back.

"Come," said the man.

The bales were up to their heads, a little higher. They were like huge bricks. He picked a bale from the top and turned to the boys. He held it out.

"Take."

Johnny stepped nearer to the man, and Tom followed him. They were under the bale now. It was too big for their arms. The man lowered it. They moved further apart. He held it between them. They put their hands out, under the bale. He let go.

"God," said Tom.

"Heavy?"

"Yeah."

"Not – heavy."

He pointed at the nearest kennel.

"Go."

They dropped the bale before they got to the kennel. But they knew what they were doing now. They carried it a bit more, and got it to the kennel. The dog came and sniffed at it.

Johnny looked back at the man. He picked up two

bales, one shoulder for each. He turned and came towards them. The dogs were whimpering again. He dropped the bales beside the boys. Johnny felt the weight of them through his boots.

He looked down at the boys. He took the knife from his belt. He wiped it on his red jacket. He looked at them, and bent down. He cut the bale twine. He didn't wear gloves. He put his fist in the straw. He pulled out a big handful. Straw twirled in the wind. Tom felt it, rough, on his cheek. The man walked up to the first kennel. He kicked the roof off it. The explosion and clatter made the dogs mad. Just for a second. The man bent down, put his other hand into the kennel. He took out old, wet straw.

He turned back to the boys. He held up the wet straw.

"Take – out."

He held up the new straw.

"Put – in."

He put the knife back in his belt.

"Jesus, lads," said Sandra when they walked into the room, an hour later. "Where are you going with that smell?"

"We were helping the man," said Tom.

"What man? Don't come in. Take your boots off first."

Sandra watched her boys take their boots off. She

could tell they were frozen. They could hardly bend their legs.

"What man was this?"

"He's in charge of the dogs."

"What's his name?"

"Don't know," said Tom. "He didn't tell us."

"Why didn't you ask him?"

"He isn't that kind of a man," said Johnny.

And Tom nodded.

"What work were you doing?" said Sandra.

"Putting straw in the kennels and stuff," said Tom. "Can we come in now?"

"I suppose so," said Sandra. "But stinky-poo, lads."

Johnny didn't like that word. It was from when he was a little kid. But he came in and got up on the bed beside Sandra.

"What are the dogs like?"

"Brilliant."

"Brilliant."

"Big day tomorrow, so?"

"Yeah.'"

They sat on the bed and told her all about the dogs, and the kennels, and the man, and the snowmobiles. But there was one thing they didn't tell her. Tom had bought a knife.

The Airport

The plane was delayed. Half an hour. EI 156. That was the name and number, and it was late.

She sat.

She'd waited all her life. Most of her life.

It was still dark outside. There weren't many people waiting. There was no one she knew or she'd ever seen before.

She sat where she could see the screens that showed the arrival times.

She took the photograph from her bag again. She put it back. She looked at the waiting people. It was getting busier.

She looked at the screen. She looked at it the same time a new word appeared: LANDED.

CHAPTER FOUR

It was very dark and very quiet. The excitement was the thing that told the boys it was morning. They woke up together, both pushed up by it.

"Is she still asleep?"

"No, she isn't," said their mother. "She's starving."

They climbed down out of their huge bunk bed and got in under their mother's duvet.

"That was the best night's sleep I ever had in my life," she said.

"So what?" said Johnny.

She tickled him out of the bed, and Tom followed him on to the floor. They got dressed quickly.

"Don't forget to put on your thermals," said Sandra.

"Ah, yes," said Tom. "Our toasty thermals."

"Our underground knickers," said Johnny.

They were dressed and ready to go.

"Can we go without you?" said Tom.

She always took ages to get ready, even when she was in a hurry.

"Sure," she said. "I'll be right behind you."

It was very quiet out in the corridor. They walked and skidded on down to the foyer place. They could smell food they thought they'd like, and then they were at the dining room. It was full of quiet people, and they both noticed it at the same time – no kids. At all. There were no children. Just Johnny and Tom.

Some people looked over at them. Some smiled. Some didn't.

"All grown-ups," said Tom.

"I'm hungry," said Johnny.

It was one of those places where you served yourself. There was a counter with cooked stuff – eggs, sausages, toast – and a table with cereal and fruit and things of yoghurt.

Johnny went to the table. There was a huge glass bowl full of muesli.

"Is that all?"

But then he saw the little boxes. Cornflakes, Rice Krispies, and one he didn't know but was covered in chocolate. He looked out to the foyer – no sign of their mother.

"Quick."

They grabbed a box of the chocolate cereal each, and a bowl and spoon. There was no empty table. They had to sit beside a man and a woman who looked way too old to be messing around with dogs and snow.

"Hello," said the man.

He smiled. There was a reindeer on the woman's jumper.

"Hello," said Tom.

"English?" said the man.

"No," said Tom.

"Irish," said Johnny.

"Ah," said the man.

He said something to the woman. She nodded. The man pointed at himself and then at the woman.

"Belgium."

"Brussels," said Tom.

"No," said the man.

Tom looked at Johnny.

"Brussels *is* in Belgium," he said. "It's the capital city of it."

"He's not from Brussels," said Johnny.

"I never said he was," said Tom. "I only told him Brussels is in Belgium."

"D'you not think he knows that already?"

"Shut up."

"Muppet."

"Thick."

"Muppet."

The man smiled. The boys opened the cereal boxes and dumped the chocolate stuff into their bowls.

"Coo-il. They're shaped like dogs."

"They're not."

"They are. Look."

"That's not a dog."

"It *is*. That's his tail, look."

"Shut up and just eat it."

By the time their mother got there, Johnny and Tom had eaten the cereal, and they'd thrown the evidence, the empty boxes, into the bin. They'd filled their plates with cooked stuff, and they were just starting to eat it.

"Looks good," she said.

Johnny's mouth was full of sausage that didn't taste as he'd expected, and he didn't know if he liked it or not. His mother was staring at his mouth. He swallowed the meat.

"Is that chocolate I see on your lips?" she said.

"No," said Johnny.

Tom quickly wiped his mouth. The no-chocolate rule was stupid. It made no sense. She let them eat everything else. She was looking at his mouth now. He could feel himself going red.

Then a man came in, right behind their mother.

"Hello," he shouted. "People!"

He was dressed in black. He had a black fleece, and big, black padded trousers. His hair was white, and he had a beard with a point on it, done in little braids, like the back of a girl's hair. And a red-and-black striped cap with the bits for the ears tied up. He was young, for a man, and he looked nice.

"Good morning, people," he said. "Everybody speaks English, yeah?"

Tom and Johnny looked around. Some of the adults nodded, and two of them said "Yes" out loud. Three of them looked down at their tables.

"Cool," said the man. "So. My name is Aki. Spells A-K-I, I guess. Finnish name, yeah? Aki. I am your GUIDE."

"Ah," said the man who wasn't from Brussels.

Other people nodded.

"And we will go now to get the suits and boots, and then we will meet the dogs."

"We met them already," said Tom.

"And good," said Aki. "You are Thomas or John?"

"Tom," said Tom.

"Awesome," said Aki. "And you are John."

"Yeah," said Johnny.

"Also awesome," said Aki. "And so."

He turned. They followed.

Sandra grabbed some toast and a sausage, and they all followed Aki out of the hotel. It was cold.

"Yum," said Sandra. "The sausage is nice."

"The meat of the deer is in the sausage," said the man from Belgium.

"Oh, Jesus," said Sandra. "Poor Bambi."

It was still dark. It was lovely, a silvery grey colour. She slid on ice, but didn't fall. She'd forgotten her gloves. Her hands were already hurting, only a few seconds after coming outside. She pushed them into her pockets, but that made walking on the ice more difficult. So, she took them out again. She could balance better now. They weren't going far, just across the yard and down a little icy hill. To a big, red-painted shed. The light from the open door cut a triangle in front of the shed.

She looked at her watch. It was nearly half-nine. She'd have been at work by now. She looked at the boys. They were like two rabbits in front of her, bobbing along; she could see the excitement in their bodies. They were keeping up with Aki, chatting away, probably driving him mad with questions.

She wondered how Frank was getting on, and Gráinne. She was glad she was here, just for a while. Just herself and the boys. Away from the complications. Fresh air and deer meat – things were nice and simple here. She was sure they were fine, Frank and Gráinne. And the mother, the ex-wife – Rosemary. What about her?

It was sudden, a shock – she slid, and fell backwards. But her head landed on the man from Belgium's boots. She was OK. Hands helped her up. She was OK, a bit embarrassed.

"You are fine?"

"Yes," she said. "I'm grand. I'm fine. Thanks."

Someone behind her slipped, and she felt less embarrassed and hot. She heard laughter. Foreign voices. She'd like this, the adventure. She was fine. She walked on.

A few minutes later, they all stood in the yard and looked huge. They were dressed in big red suits that made them all look a bit like astronauts. They had scarves and gloves, either red ones made from the same stuff as the suits, or caps and gloves of their own. There was lots of laughing and back slapping. Aki gave them time to take photographs of one another.

"Stand still a minute, lads," said Sandra.

But they didn't. Running properly wasn't easy because the suits were so fat and stiff. But the boys were able to run slowly, and they ran straight into each other – and bounced. They were padded, and it didn't hurt, not when they whacked into each other, not even when they landed on the hard snow. They made the noise –

"Ouch, ouch!"

"Agon-eee!"

But they were fine. They got up to do it again, but then they heard the dogs, and that was more important.

And Aki thought so too.

"And SO," he said. "We go."

The big red people turned and followed Aki. Tom and Johnny knew the way, and they rushed and skidded ahead of him. They blew the steam that came from their mouths straight into each other's faces.

"Killer steam! Die, small boy!"

They were at the dogs again, in among the kennels and the smell. The dogs were excited, and none of them were standing on the kennel roofs. They knew they were going out; Johnny and Tom could tell.

"So, these are the husky dogs, I guess," said Aki. "And, hey, I think they like you."

He was talking to Johnny and Tom, and they were delighted. They looked at their mother. She was smiling at them.

"So," said Aki. "People."

He waited for the last of the adults to arrive. The man who wasn't from Brussels had stood on poo and was trying to rub it off on the snow. And that was stupid because the snow was full of it already.

"So," said Aki, again. "These are your huskies. For four days, I guess."

Johnny decided; Aki was good at his job. He was scaring them a bit, but he was making them much more excited, the way he shouted some words and whispered others.

"Look at the eyes," said Aki. "AWESOME."

And the adults who hadn't noticed, noticed now.

"Oh, look, lads," said their mother. "They're gorgeous."

"Very beautiful," said the not-from-Brussels man. "You agree?" he asked Johnny.

Johnny nodded. He didn't want to be rude. But he'd seen the eyes already, and he just wanted to go.

"Too beautiful, I think," said the woman from Belgium.

"I know what you mean," said their mother. "You could never trust a fella with eyes like those."

What was she on about now? What would a fella be doing with a dog's eyes?

But Aki finished the eyetime.

"So," he said. "How will these dogs bring us on the safari?"

No one answered. None of the adults wanted to be wrong, even though the answer was easy.

"On the backs?"

Some of the adults laughed.

"No," said Tom.

"With saddles?"

"I said, no," said Tom.

"Right," said Aki. "I am being a dumb-ass, yeah?"

"Yeah," said Tom.

"Tom," said his mother.

"Sorry," said Tom.

"For sure," said Aki. "So. How?"

He was looking at Tom.

"Sleigh," said Johnny.

"Me," said Tom. "Sledge."

"Right and right," said Aki. "Sleigh and sledge."

"There is a difference?"

"No."

"Oh."

"Or sled," said Aki. "Three words for one thing. CHOOSE."

He pointed at Tom, then Johnny.

"Sled!" they said, together.

"Good choice," said Aki. "Cool. How many dogs?"

"What do you mean?" said Johnny.

"To pull the sleigh and sledge and sled. Each. How many dogs?"

"Four?"

"Right," said Aki. "So."

Tom and Johnny saw the panic on the adult faces; their brains were catching up. Four mad dogs to master and control. Four dogs to mush-mush. Four dogs to point in the right direction and hope that they would go that way.

"So," said Aki. "This way."

He walked across to the nearest sled. They all followed him. No one was laughing now; no one was talking. They stopped when he stopped.

"Come," he said.

They gathered around the sled. There were no dogs attached to it yet. It was a very simple thing, made mostly from wood that looked like very thick, shiny string. There were two runners, parallel, at the bottom, with a thin plate made of metal on each runner, to stand on. There was a bar across the back of the sled, just over the runners.

Aki stood on the runners.

"See?"

He put a foot down on the bar, and they heard it scrape the ice. Aki got off the sled and picked it up. Beneath the bar, they saw a jagged line of steel, like serious teeth or a bear trap.

"The brake," he said.

"Cool," said Johnny.

"Right," said Aki.

He dropped the sled and stood on it again. He put his foot on the bar, and the steel teeth bit into the ice.

"Doesn't work so well in ice, I guess," he said. "But in snow, put your foot down. The sleigh or sled will stop. I promise this, no problems."

He picked up the sled with one hand.

"Not heavy."

He put it down again.

"And the reins?" said the man from Belgium.

"What say?" said Aki.

The man pretended he was riding a horse. He even click-clicked with his mouth.

"No reins," said Aki.

"How will the dogs know?" said the man.

"Know what?"

"To go," said the man.

"They will know," said Aki.

He looked at all of them.

"And you MUST also know," he said.

He held the handles.

"Hands here, feet here. No problem."

Johnny looked at all the adult faces. "But," the faces said. "Who, me?" they said. "I wish I was in Spain."

But no one spoke. It was up to Johnny, and Tom.

"How do we make them go?" said Johnny.

"You do not make them go. Tom?"

"Johnny."

"Right. You and – Tom?"

"Yeah."

"You are very young, I guess," said Aki. "You will go with Kalle."

"Who's that?" said Johnny.

The Belgian man tapped Johnny on the shoulder.

"This is him, I think."

And they saw him.

No one spoke.

Kalle was the man Johnny and Tom had met the day before. He was still very tall and very wide, and he still had the knife on his belt.

"So, good morning, Kalle," said Aki.

Kalle didn't answer, but he nodded at Aki. He walked past all the adults, to the dogs.

He still wasn't wearing a hat.

"So, this is Kalle," said Aki. "Kalle is the dog man."

"He owns them?"

"Right."

He pointed at Kalle. Kalle was collecting strips of leather, pulling the strips, making sure they wouldn't snap. Tom had seen the leather strips the day before. They were the things that held the huskies to the sleds.

"Kalle is how you get your dogs to go," said Aki. "The dogs will follow Kalle."

He smiled.

"Four dogs for each."

He patted the Belgian man's stomach as he passed him.

"Five for you, perhaps," he said.

The Belgian man laughed, but his wife or girlfriend looked annoyed.

Aki winked at Johnny and Tom.

"Come," he said.

He showed them how to get the harness over a dog's head. He let them do it. And the dogs let them do it. The dogs licked their hands as they put the leather straps over their ears. It was easy.

They looked around. They were way ahead of the adults. Some of them stood there, holding the harnesses, as if they were going to put them over their own heads. Their mother couldn't decide which end of the harness to start with.

The dogs licking their hands was a sign of friendliness, Aki told them. "And," he said, "when the dog puts your hand in the mouth, it's cool. He likes you."

"Just as well," said Johnny. "Look."

The husky had Johnny's gloved hand in his mouth. Johnny could feel the teeth through the cloth, but the dog wasn't pressing them into his hand.

Tom put his hand in front of his dog's mouth, and the dog took it.

"How do you do?" he said.

He patted the dog's head. The ears sprang back up. They were like little triangles stuck on top of its head. He did it again. The ears sprang up again.

The harness went around the dog's mouth, across the snout. The dogs let it happen; they didn't pull back or snarl. Tom's dog even pushed its head forward, to help him get the harness on. Aki bent down and helped him tighten the strap a bit, so the harness wouldn't slip over the dog's head.

Tom looked around again. The woman from Belgium was sitting down. Her reindeer hat was in a dog's mouth. She was laughing. His mother had her arm around her dog's neck. She was laughing too, but she was grunting a bit as well.

"So," said Aki.

Everybody looked. Some of the dogs looked.

The big man was standing beside Aki. Aki looked small beside him. Kalle didn't nod or say hello. He just stood.

"Kalle wears a hat only when the temperature goes under minus thirty," said Aki.

Tom and Johnny heard gasps.

"If Kalle wears a hat, it is very cold. You need two hats."

Kalle hadn't budged since Aki had started talking. Johnny wondered if he could understand what Aki was saying.

"Kalle shows you how to hitch the husky dog to the sleigh or sled."

And, before Aki had finished speaking, Kalle grabbed the collar of Johnny's dog and pulled the dog over to the sled. The dog didn't object or pull back. He went side by side with Kalle.

Kalle picked up a leather strap. It was long, and attached to the front of Kalle's sled. The sled was bigger and longer than the others; it would have eight dogs to pull it. Kalle brought this dog to the front of the long strap. Then he clipped two side straps to the dog, to the collar, and to the harness. He grabbed another dog, and led him – or her; Tom wasn't sure if it was a boy or a girl – and put him beside the first, on the other side of the long strap.

Aki pointed at the first dog.

"This dog," he said.

He patted the dog.

"This husky dog is the lead dog," said Aki. "He leads, I guess. He is the boss of the husky dogs. And Kalle is the boss of him. He goes where Kalle wants him to go. The other husky dogs follow him."

Aki brought up his hands and moved them, as if he was flicking reins.

"So," he said. "No reins, yeah? The husky dogs will follow this one, even if you hold reins and go mush-mush."

"What's his name?" said Tom.

Kalle spoke for the first time that morning.

"Rock," he said.

It was the perfect name. Even the adults thought so. They looked less worried. The man from Belgium nodded.

"A good name," he said.

"Yeah," said Johnny.

"A good dog."

"Yeah."

Tom liked the dogs' tails. They were bushy, and curved over their backs. It was the tails that told Tom the dogs were happy and excited. They knew they were going for a run.

Gradually, all the dogs were hitched to the sleds. It took a while with their mother. One of her dogs was a messer.

"Ah," said Aki. "The famous Hastro."

He grabbed the dog, to help their mother. The dog had two different coloured eyes, a brown and a blue.

"Why is he famous?" said Johnny.

"He is not famous," said Aki. "But he wants to be, I guess."

He patted the dog.

"Is that right, Hastro?"

He backed the dog into place, and hooked the strap to his harness. Then he stood up straight and stepped back.

"Hastro thinks he is the lead dog," he said.

"Oh, God," said their mother. "One of those ones. Can I not just have a harmless eejit?"

Aki laughed.

"Eejit?" he said. "What is eejit?"

Johnny pointed at Tom.

"Him," he said. "He's an eejit."

Tom hated that. He hated when his brother stopped being his best friend, and became nasty. He hated when it happened; he never saw it coming.

He blinked back the tears.

"Johnny," said his mother.

"Sorry," said Johnny.

"To Tom," said his mother.

She put her arms around both boys.

"Sorry," said Johnny.

Tom nodded. He wasn't going to cry now. Did tears freeze? He wouldn't find out.

Their mother held them for a bit longer, until she felt them getting restless. They were fine again. She let them go. They walked over to Kalle's sled. They didn't look back at their mother.

The adults stood on the sleds. They stood on the

brakes at the back. There were four dogs for each sled, two on each side of the long strap. Some of the dogs pulled a bit, but not too hard. They wanted to go. They wanted to run.

The boys looked around. Their mother waved at them. She looked a bit nervous, taking her hand off the sled.

Aki stood near the boys.

"Why can't we have a sled of our own?" said Johnny.

"Each," said Tom.

"Guys," said Aki. "You are too young."

"That's stupid," said Tom.

"Everybody always says that," said Johnny. "Is being young a criminal offence or something?"

"I explain," said Aki. "You are not too young, OK? But too light. Not enough of the kilos on the brake, yeah."

He stamped his foot.

"The brake doesn't work. The husky dogs bring you to Russia."

He pointed.

"East," he said. "Not good."

"I thought they all followed Rock," said Johnny.

"Yes," said Aki. "But you need the kilos for the brake. Guys, I'm sorry."

They were annoyed and disappointed, but they knew he was right. He was being honest. They both liked him.

"Where's your sled?" said Tom.

"There is no sleigh or sled for Aki," said Aki. "I travel in style."

He pointed at a snowmobile.

"Why?" said Tom.

Aki waved one of his hands, left to right, and back.

"I go forward and backward. People fall off the sleigh or sled, I pick them up. I reunite them with the sleigh or sled. I go ahead and make the fire for the coffee."

"What coffee?"

"There is no husky safari without coffee," said Aki.

"That's stupid," said Tom.

Aki lifted his hands.

"Guys," he said. "It is my job. People like the coffee in the wilderness."

They liked the sound of that word. Wilderness. They looked at each other and grinned.

Kalle stood beside his sled. He didn't need to stand on his brake. His dogs wouldn't run away. Tom and Johnny went over to him. They were to sit beside each other, in front of Kalle, in a narrow hollow. They climbed in. They sat back. They were nearly lying down.

"Move over," said Johnny.

"Move over, yourself," said Tom.

They pushed each other.

"Lads," they heard their mother. "Behave yourselves."

"He started it," said Tom.

Johnny pinched him, but Tom hardly felt it because of all his padding. But he thumped Johnny. And Johnny thumped Tom. It could have gone on like that for ever if Kalle hadn't stopped it.

They saw Kalle's face coming closer to them. They stayed absolutely still as the face came down from high above them. They saw the black stubble on his chin. They saw one big black hair sticking out of his nostril. They saw the nose that looked hard enough to batter its way through solid rock.

They saw his eyes. Kalle stared at them. For a long time.

No one was talking. No dogs were whimpering. The wind wasn't shaking the trees.

Kalle spoke.

"Your – country?" he said.

"Ireland," said Johnny.

"In – Ireland," said Kalle, "children – obey – the – mothers. Yes?'

"Yes," said Johnny.

"Yes," said Tom.

"Yes," said Kalle.

His face rose over them. They could see the trees again, and they heard people move and cough. Kalle was standing up again. He held a blanket as thick as a rug. He flapped it, and it dropped gently on to Johnny and Tom. Kalle was bending again as he tucked the blanket around the boys. They didn't want it – they weren't in a hospital or something – but they didn't say anything.

"Thanks," said Johnny when Kalle was finished.

Kalle didn't answer.

"SO," said Aki. "We go."

Suddenly, Johnny and Tom were moving, fast. They started laughing. They were gliding over the snow, behind eight dogs. The dogs went straight for the gate. Out the gate, and they saw more snow than they'd ever seen before. More snow than they'd even imagined.

Johnny had to do it; he couldn't stop. He had to shout – it was so exciting.

"Wilderness!"

And Tom joined in, like an echo.

"Wil-der-ness!!"

The Airport

People were pouring out now. She saw women and men shake hands, or hug. A woman stopped in front of her. She looked uncertain, and unhappy. She took a piece of paper from her pocket. She looked at it. She looked around, at the faces all around her. She moved a bit; she dragged the luggage trolley with her. She looked round again. She began to look angry.

It wasn't her mother.

Too young – she looked.

Too angry.

Gráinne was scared she'd miss her, that she'd missed her already, that she'd gone past Gráinne while Gráinne was looking the wrong way. She looked behind her. There were more people waiting. Most of them were like her, waiting for someone off a plane. But there were others leaning on trolleys, sitting on bags, standing, waiting to be met or recognised. They were talking into mobile phones, and texting. They were tired and pale, and some of them were nearly crying.

She turned and saw more people pour into the arrivals hall. A man and woman in wheelchairs were met and quickly surrounded by a gang of people. They laughed and shouted. They annoyed her; they got in the way. They were too happy, and she couldn't see around them, or over their heads. She was afraid she'd miss her mother. There were too many people to stare at; they wouldn't move slowly. It was too confusing.

"Gráinne?"

Gráinne stood there.

"Is it Gráinne?"

"Yes," said Gráinne.

"Hello."

The woman who stood there was her mother. She was the woman in the photograph – her eyes, and the way her hair was on her forehead. She was the same.

Gráinne didn't know what to do.

She'd expected to feel suddenly full, lost time charging back into her – she didn't know. She'd expected it to feel right. But, now, she felt nothing. It was like there was a wall in the way. Waiting had been much easier.

She wanted to run away. She didn't – she did. She just didn't know.

She didn't run.

"Hi," she said.

"It's – gosh," said the woman. "It's so great to see you. And thanks for meeting me."

What did she mean? Why wouldn't Gráinne have met her?

Maybe her mother saw the questions race over Gráinne's face.

"Here," she explained. "Thanks for meeting me *here*. The first person I meet when I come home. You. It's –"

She laughed. But it wasn't a real laugh.

"It's perfect," she said.

She smiled. Her eyes were wet.

"Sorry," she said. "I'll shut up. I told myself not to talk too much."

She'd never heard this woman's voice before. It wasn't in Gráinne's memory. Nothing clicked, or came back. She'd looked nice in the photograph. She looked nice here too.

"I like your bag," said her mother.

Gráinne looked at her bag. It was just a bag. Plain and black, like a sack.

She shrugged.

"It's a bit like mine," said her mother.

But she didn't have a bag. She'd cases and stuff piled on a trolley. It was hard to tell if she'd come home for good, or just for a visit. Gráinne couldn't see a shoulderbag.

"I mean," said her mother. "I have one a bit like yours."

"Oh," said Gráinne. "Cool."

"It's in the mess, somewhere," said her mother.

She smiled again.

"It's quite crowded here," she said. "Will we go somewhere?"

"Are you not staying with Granny?"

"Yes," said her mother. "I mean, before that. We could go somewhere, for breakfast. Just the two of us."

"OK," said Gráinne.

"Where?" said her mother. "It's been years. I don't remember anywhere nice in Dublin."

Gráinne didn't like choosing. She was no good at it. She didn't know nice places.

"I know," said her mother. "We'll take a cab to your granny's, and I'll leave the bags there. And then we can go somewhere. For breakfast. Sound good?"

She sounded American. Just a little bit. *Sound good?* Gráinne liked it – and she didn't. It made her mother even more foreign.

"OK," said Gráinne.

"Grand," said her mother. And that sounded Irish.

She started to push her trolley. Then she stopped.

"Do you want to call me Rosemary?" she said. "You probably don't want to call me –"

She laughed again, that nervous laugh.

"What did I call you?" said Gráinne.

"What?"

"What did I call you?" said Gráinne. "I don't remember."

She watched her mother try to smile. She watched the smile turn crooked and break up. She saw her close her eyes. She heard her.

"I'm – sorry."

They looked at each other.

"Mama," said her mother. "That's what you called me."

CHAPTER FIVE

It was a white path. It was long and straight, and it disappeared as they went over it. The sleds were going faster than a car – that was what it felt like. And they were nearer the ground; they could feel it right under them. They could hear the runners, the blades, beneath them. They could hear them scratch and glide over the ice.

They looked straight ahead. At the dogs.

The dogs didn't gallop. They didn't lift their legs and throw them back, the way horses seemed to, pushing themselves forward. The dogs trotted, little steps, like they weren't in that big a hurry. The boys had seen dogs on Dollymount beach, charging across the sand, tongues out, heads down to the level of their backs. But these dogs weren't like that. They couldn't be; they were tied to the sled. But Tom and Johnny knew: if they had been ordinary dogs, they'd have been pulling too fast, bashing into each other, getting themselves caught in the straps.

They were coming to a hill.

These weren't ordinary dogs. They were working together. They had to save their energy, so they didn't dash. They pulled and charged a bit at the start, to get the sled moving. But then they calmed down. Rock, the leader, didn't look at them or howl. But he slowed down, and so did they.

But that was the thing. They didn't slow down. They were going like crazy. When Johnny looked to the side it was a white blur, and a bit scary. Then he looked straight ahead again, and the dogs were just trotting away, their breath steaming out. They were much, much stronger than their size. Their tails were up, and their breath was like laughter.

The hill was nearer. It wasn't that high. The boys saw Aki on his snowmobile, on top of the hill. He was waving, telling them to come forward. Tom tried to look behind, at Kalle, to see if he was waving back. But he couldn't turn properly. He was afraid he'd fall out of the sled; it was bouncing a bit on the ice.

The dogs started up the hill.

Aki kept waving. They could hear him.

"Come, come! No cars!"

They saw it now; the top of the hill was a road. They went past Aki, and straight across. They looked left and right. The road was straight and empty. It was a scar, right through the white forest. It was daytime now, but the air was silver. The sky was low enough to touch.

The road was ending.

"Oh, oh."

They laughed. They could feel their guts getting ready. They were going to drop. The dogs ran down the hill on the other side of the road; they didn't slow down or hesitate. And Tom and Johnny were right behind them. The path was gone. There *was* a path, but it was narrow now, and never straight. They were right in the forest and going over big snow. They swerved around rocks and trees. They pushed into each other as they turned; they couldn't help it. They leaned out over the side of the sled. They couldn't help that either. The dogs still trotted along, like this was normal. They watched the dogs, and they felt normal too.

This was the best thing that had ever happened to them. They both thought that, at the same time.

The sled swerved, and they couldn't see the dogs for a second – they were off the ground, and then they were behind the dogs again. There was a path, but only because the dogs were running on it. Johnny and Tom couldn't really see it. The trees were green here. They were in dark forest, away from the edge. This was wilderness. They both felt it – they knew. This was where you could get lost – really lost. Something had changed. They didn't just like the dogs. They needed them.

They could hear their dogs panting. They could

hear the other dogs behind them. They could hear the runners on the snow. They could hear Aki's snowmobile.

They went between two big trees, and the land opened in front of them. It was a wide, white space, like a small park or a football pitch, flat and silvery white. They could see the silver sky again. But the wall of the forest was straight ahead. They were going to go back in.

They heard dog breath and paws, right behind them. Johnny looked back, but he couldn't see anything. Tom looked, and saw four dogs running towards him, coming up, about to pass them. They were pulling an empty sled. It was bouncing around a bit, jumping, because it was so light.

But the dogs didn't pass Kalle's sled.

"They won't pass the leader," said Johnny. "That's why they've slowed down."

"Oh, yeah," said Tom.

He heard Kalle shout something, over their heads. Something short. One word, one syllable. That was all, and the dogs in front slowed and stopped. Tom felt the weight behind him; Kalle was standing on the brake.

The other dogs stopped too. Kalle walked through the snow to the other sled. He patted the front dogs. They rubbed against his arm. They moaned and muttered happily.

"Come on," said Johnny.

He pulled back the blanket and climbed out of the sled. Tom thought about this. There was no reason for them not to do it. It wasn't dangerous, and they weren't at school. So, he got out from under the blanket too. He could make out lots of sled tracks, and some paw prints. The snow wasn't thick. But when he stood up and took a few steps away from the sled, the snow went up his boots, right up to the tops. It was great.

Kalle looked at Tom and Johnny. He said nothing. They stood beside him and watched Aki come towards them on the snowmobile. There was someone else on the snowmobile, behind him.

It was their mother.

"She must have fallen off," said Tom.

"Cool," said Johnny.

The snowmobile slowed as it got nearer the dogs, and stopped. Their mother got off the back. They saw her stretch to get her foot over the seat. She nearly fell. They could see her face. She was red. She looked at Tom and Johnny. She smiled at them and stuck out her tongue. She struggled through the high snow. Then one of her feet landed on the hardened snow, and she saw that it was easier to walk on the path.

"Hiya, lads," she said. "I went on my bum."

They laughed.

Kalle spoke.

"Why – did – you – fall – off – your – sleigh?" he said.

"Ah Jaysis, Kalle," said their mother. "I didn't do it on purpose."

They could hear Aki laughing.

"What – was – the – cause?" said Kalle.

"I – don't – know," said their mother. "I – just – fell – off."

She lifted her hands.

"Sorry," she said. "I'm being rude. Sorry, Kalle. But I just fell off."

Kalle nodded.

"*Paska* – happens," he said.

The other sleds had caught up. Johnny could see the other people trying to stay steady on their brakes. Their dogs tried to pull, nearer to Kalle.

"And, so," said Aki.

They heard him turn on the snowmobile.

Kalle held their mother's sled while she stepped on to it and put her feet on the brake. He turned and stared at Tom, and Johnny.

They ran – they tried to run – back to the sled, through the high snow, then the flattened stuff. Tom slid. He tried it again, but it didn't work. Johnny got there first.

"Sorry, no room."

He pushed Tom back.

"Lay off," said Tom.

He slid again. But this time he didn't want to. He tried to get on to the sled, and Johnny pushed again.

Suddenly, Kalle was there. He leaned down and picked up Johnny. He hoisted him a few centimetres and dropped him to the side. There was room for Tom. He climbed in.

"Brothers," said Kalle. "I – understand."

"Do you have a brother?" said Tom.

"I – give – him – to – the – husky – dogs," said Kalle. "They – eat."

"Really?"

Kalle nodded.

Tom believed him. He didn't – he did. There was nothing jokey about Kalle. But maybe Finnish jokes weren't meant to be funny.

Kalle stepped on to the sled, behind them. He spoke to the dogs, and the sled began to move.

The Taxi

Gráinne looked out the window. Her mother was at the front door, waiting. Her cases and stuff were all around her. She leaned over one case and rang the bell again. She looked back at Gráinne and smiled.

Gráinne saw the door open. Her granny came out to the porch and hugged her mother. She saw them hold each other for a long while. She saw them speak. Her granny looked at the taxi. She smiled, and waved. Gráinne waved back.

She watched her granny and her mother bending down and picking up the cases.

"What's the story there?" said the taxi driver.

She'd forgotten he was there.

"What?" she said.

She could see his eyes in the rearview mirror. His glasses were on a bit crooked. She looked away.

She saw her mother coming out of the house. She

turned, and said something to Gráinne's granny. She waved, and started walking to the taxi.

"Is that your mother?" said the taxi driver.

Gráinne didn't answer.

CHAPTER SIX

They were going over ice now. They were on a lake, just a few centimetres between them and the freezing water.

Tom pulled back his head and called up to Kalle.

"Is it deep?"

"Not – understand," said Kalle.

His voice boomed across the ice. The trees at the lakeside seemed to shake.

"Is there much water?" said Johnny.

He pointed at the ice.

Kalle nodded.

There were branches and sticks poking out of the ice. They marked the safe path across the lake, where the ice was thickest. It was like a race now, like the skiing they'd seen on telly. The dogs went right between the sticks. Sometimes they skidded, but it didn't slow down or confuse them.

Aki went past them, on the snowmobile. He hit one

of the marker branches but it didn't snap or fall. It sprang back to the upright position.

"The ice must be thick," said Tom.

He had to say it loud. The sky seemed to swallow up his voice.

"Yeah," said Johnny.

They were safe, but it was still exciting. Ice melted; ice broke. Some messers might have changed the positions of the sticks and sent the sled the wrong and dangerous way.

They sailed over the ice.

They went past a house. It was suddenly there, at the edge of the lake, like a story house. It was wood and painted green. It seemed to move beside them, and then they left it behind.

Johnny looked back, but the house was gone, hidden by the trees. He was cold. His face was very cold. He hadn't moved in hours. He saw Aki ahead of them. The snowmobile went over a hump and into the trees. Aki was off the lake. Johnny couldn't see him now. Just before the dogs reached the lakeside, he saw a wide gap in the trees, and he could see the sun. He could see half the sun, like the top half of a big red eye, staring at him.

"Is that the sun or the moon?" said Tom.

"Sun," said Johnny.

"How do you know?" said Tom.

"Shut up," said Johnny.

The dogs climbed the bank. One of them slipped but was held up by the others and the harness. They dragged the sled up, off the ice. They were in among the trees again, and the wind was off their faces. But they were still cold, that shivery feeling that takes ages to go away. The light had changed. It was darker here. The trees closed in above them, and the light was cut into long lines that got thinner, until the sled went deeper into the trees, and they left the light behind.

Then they saw the fire.

The dogs headed for it. They swerved among the trees, but always, when the turn was finished, the fire was in front of them.

They came out of the trees, to a small clearing with a frozen stream and snow-hidden bushes and silver light that seemed solid enough to climb.

Aki was sitting at the fire, on a log. He waved as Kalle called over the boys' heads, and the dogs stopped. The sled stopped completely. Two of the dogs lay down. The boys started to climb off the sled.

"Wait," said Aki.

Kalle walked past them and tied a strap to one of the small trees that grew beside the stream.

"OK," said Aki.

They got off the sled and stood up. They were stiff.

"Oh, me poor bones," said Johnny.

Tom began to jump up and down.

"Good idea," said Aki.

But they stopped, because Aki was cutting wood and that was much more interesting. He was slicing the top of a branch, again and again, making it look like a pineapple or a mad haircut.

"Burns better, I guess," he said. "See?"

He held the branch close to the fire, and the cut pieces of the branch lit quickly. The boys watched the flame spread up through the branch.

"Cool," said Tom.

He wanted to take his knife out; it was hidden in one of his pockets. But he knew his mother would have gone mad if she'd seen it.

The air was full of panting dogs and excited people. Aki and Kalle helped everyone to tie their sleds. The dogs all sat or lay in the snow. They curled up and let themselves sink in. They hid their noses under their tails.

Tom and Johnny took off their gloves and put their hands out, over the flames. They sat down on a log. There were four logs, in a square; seats around the fire.

"Luxury," said Tom.

"Move over, lads," said their mother.

She got in between them. She pretended she was pushing them away.

"What did you think?" she said.

"Brilliant," said Tom.

"Why can't we have our own sleds?" said Johnny.

"They told you—" she started.

"It's boring," said Johnny.

"Boring?" she said. "Boring?"

She picked up a stick and shook it.

"Come here till I give you boring."

Johnny ran, and she ran after him. He dived on to the snow. She sat on top of him.

"Is it boring?" she said.

"Yeah."

She picked up a handful of snow. She put it to his nose.

"Is it boring?" she said.

Tom could hear Johnny laughing.

"Yeah," said Johnny. "It's very boring."

His mother's back was blocking Tom's view, but he thought she was shoving some of the snow down Johnny's back.

"Is it boring?" he heard her.

"Stop!"

"Is it boring?"

"No!"

He shouted so loud a small bird shot out of a bush beside him.

Tom laughed.

"Siberian jay," said Aki. "This bird is the soul of a dead hunter."

"Really?" said Tom.

"For sure."

Tom heard his mother.

"Is it exciting?"

"Yes!" Johnny yelled.

"How exciting?"

"Stop!"

"*How* exciting?"

"The best ever!"

"Great," said his mother.

She stood up. She hugged Johnny when he was standing up. Tom wanted to go over there now, to throw snow, and be chased and hugged.

The man from Belgium was sitting now, near Tom.

"Your mother," he said.

He pointed, and smiled.

"Is a very attractive woman," he said.

Tom knew his face was turning red. He wanted to jump up and hit the man from Belgium. But his wife or girlfriend was sitting beside him, and she nodded too. She leaned out, so she could look properly at Tom.

"She is very nice," she said. "The way she plays with your brother."

The man nodded. And that was fine. He just thought Tom's mother was nice. And that was OK. Because she was.

"Tom?" he heard Aki.

Tom looked. Aki was at the fire, kneeling beside it.

"Will you help?" said Aki.

"OK," said Tom.

Would he help? He went so quickly, he nearly tripped and dived into the fire. He landed right beside Aki. Aki was cutting a thin branch at the top, to make it split in two. He had tied three other thin branches together, using a strip of bark. They stood like a teepee, or the legs of a stool.

"See how I cut?" he said.

"Yeah," said Tom.

Aki handed the knife to Tom. It was like one of the knives in the showcase, and way bigger than the knife Tom had hidden in his pocket. Aki was holding it out for Tom. He wasn't telling him to be careful or anything. Tom took the knife; he held the handle. It wasn't as cold as he'd expected, probably because Aki had been holding it. It was quite heavy. He looked around. He hoped Johnny was watching, and his mother too.

They were. They were looking at him. They were coming towards the fire. He pretended he hadn't been looking at them. He turned, back to Aki.

Aki was holding the stick he'd been splitting.

"See why I do this?" said Aki.

"Yeah," said Tom.

"Why?" said Aki.

"Eh, not sure."

"Cut it a bit more," said Aki. "Then I show you."

"OK."

"What are you doing?"

It was Johnny.

"Helping Aki," said Tom.

"How?" said Johnny.

"We are making the coffee," said Aki.

Tom was careful with the knife. This was his chance; he wasn't being treated like a baby. He cut a bigger notch at the tip of the branch. He made sure the sharp side wasn't facing his fingers and body. He knew how to do it. He knew he was being watched.

"Let's see," said Johnny.

Tom knew what that meant. Johnny didn't want to see the knife. He wanted Tom to give it to him. Tom ignored him.

"Give us a go," said Johnny.

Tom could feel Johnny leaning into him. But he knew that Johnny wouldn't grab the knife, not in front of Aki and their mother.

"Next time, you," said Aki, to Johnny.

That was fine with Tom. He was the first one to use a real hunter's knife.

"That is good," said Aki. "And, OK."

Tom stopped cutting. He didn't have to be told again. He handed the stick to Aki. He held the knife. He did nothing with it. He just held it, like it was a pen or a ruler or something normal from his life. He watched Aki put the branch across the other tree branches, the ones he'd already tied. He made it lean across the top of the branches. It was now hanging over the centre of the fire.

"See?" said Aki.

"Yeah," said Johnny.

"And, now," said Aki.

He lifted the branch off the other branches.

"You will see why you cut the wood."

He picked up the coffeepot. It was like one of those old-fashioned pots from a Western film. It was made of tin and had a handle at the top. Aki pushed the handle between the two split parts of the branch top. Then he held the branch and put it hanging over the fire again, with the coffeepot right in the middle. He sat back on one of the log seats and put the end of the branch under his foot. The pot was on top of the fire, but the branch was too high above to catch fire.

"That's brilliant," said Tom's mother.

"It will take a very long time?" said the man from Belgium.

"Not so long, I guess," said Aki.

They all sat on the logs around the fire, squashed into each other. They were very cold, but a bit too tired to notice. They waited for the coffee; they held the wooden cups Aki had handed them. The sweat was drying inside their suits. Their arms were still shaking, from holding on to the sleds. Their hands were sweaty and aching. They sat in the silver, slanting sunlight. The heat of the fire lifted the smell of strong coffee to their noses. They knew this was special. They loved what they'd just done, and most of them dreaded doing it again in a few minutes. Some people spoke quietly to each other, and most were happy to stay quiet.

"Boring!"

It was Johnny, and he let himself fall backwards off the log, so he'd land on the snow and get out of the squash of adult shoulders. Tom followed him. They stood up together and ran straight at the deep snow.

Johnny stopped.

"Are there any snakes here?" he asked.

"Some, I guess," said Aki. "Adder. Bushmaster. Cobra."

He shrugged.

"It's OK," he said. "It's cool. They sleep, I think."

Johnny looked at Tom.

They ran.

The snow got deeper and deeper. Ankles, shins, knees, over the knees. They ran past the dogs. They had to lift their legs higher.

"Jump," said Johnny. "One, two . . . three!"

They jumped out of the hold of the snow. They lifted their arms; they stretched them out. They stuck out their chests. They hit the snow.

The Café

Her mother put the tray on the table. She took off her coat and put it on the back of her chair. Then she sat down. She smiled and looked away, then looked again at Gráinne.

"Well," she said.

Gráinne said nothing. What was she supposed to say?

She took a bite out of her Danish; she was starving. But her mother started taking the things off the tray, and Gráinne knew she'd started too early. She hated this. She'd been rude, but she didn't know why.

She helped her mother. She took the milk jug off the tray and held it up while her mother took the tray away, and leaned it against one of the table legs. She put the jug on her mother's side. She'd been going to order coffee. It would have looked better than the cardboard cup of Coke she had in front of her. Coke for breakfast was childish and not the way Gráinne wanted to be. But she'd thought that coffee might make her feel sick.

She felt a bit sick already.

She was being like a kid. She was thinking like a kid.

Maybe that was what happened, when you were with your mother. You felt like a kid. She didn't know. She didn't like it. Her arms felt rubbery. She knew she'd spill the Coke. She wanted to get up and leave. She wanted to turn the table over, to get it done with. To spill it all – all over her mother.

But she didn't. She didn't feel that way.

It was like a fight. A fight going on inside her.

"It's changed," said her mother.

"What's changed?" said Gráinne.

She was pleased with the way she said it.

"Dublin," said her mother.

"But you only got here," said Gráinne.

She felt the anger; she swallowed it back. She didn't want it to wreck the day – and everything. She knew she couldn't stop being angry. But she wanted to be in charge of it. And she didn't really feel angry now.

"I know," said her mother. "I'm being a bit stupid. It's just, I haven't been here all these years and –"

Gráinne resisted. She didn't say, "I know."

"And," said her mother. "It's just, it hits you immediately. The changes."

She stopped stirring the sugar into her coffee. She tapped the saucer with the spoon, once, twice. Gráinne watched her pick up the coffee.

"Even this," said her mother.

She held up the cup.

"You couldn't get a proper cup of coffee when I –"

She stopped.

"What?" said Gráinne. She didn't say, "Ran away," or "Deserted me". She didn't exhale loudly.

"When I lived here," said her mother.

She looked at Gráinne for a while, properly.

"Sorry," she said.

She took a sip from her cup. She took the cup away.

"I suppose everything we say – or at least I say – will be a bit of a minefield. Do you know what I mean?"

Gráinne nodded.

"But," said her mother, "it's true. You couldn't get a good cup of coffee. This is lovely."

She said "lovely" the Irish way. Gráinne drank some of her Coke. It calmed her down, the cold. It spread through her.

Her mother was looking at her again.

"Tell me a bit about yourself, Gráinne," she said.

"No," said Gráinne.

Her mother looked shocked, and suddenly like a mother.

"I don't want to," said Gráinne. "That's just crap. It's like a crap film."

Her mother still looked shocked.

"I could say the same thing to you," said Gráinne. "Tell me about yourself. It's horrible."

"Well, you know," said her mother. "You've actually told me quite a lot about yourself, just there."

Gráinne wanted to lean across and hit her. She thought she was being clever. But Gráinne only wanted to be honest. She wanted this woman to listen, to what she was saying and what she was going to say. Not what she *thought* Gráinne was saying. She'd no right. She didn't know Gráinne.

Gráinne stopped herself.

She wanted to know this woman. She really did. She had to stay calm. She tried to do it.

"You'll find out what I'm like," she said.

She shrugged.

"You're right," said her mother. "But do you mind if I tell you a bit about me?"

Gráinne shrugged again.

"If you like."

"Well," said her mother. "You know I live in New York."

Gráinne nodded. But this was weird.

"Where?" she said.

"Where, what?"

"Where in New York?" said Gráinne.

"Manhattan," said her mother. "The Upper West Side."

Gráinne nodded. She'd imagined herself there. All her life she'd seen herself walking down one of the streets. Or, since she'd found out where her mother lived.

"What number street?" she said.

"One hundred and sixteenth," said her mother. "And Amsterdam."

She lived near the corner of one hundred and sixteenth Street and Amsterdam Avenue. Streets across, avenues up and down. Gráinne had seen maps of New York on the internet. She'd printed one out. It was on her bedroom wall.

"Do you live in an apartment?" she asked.

"Yes," said her mother. "They don't have houses like here."

Gráinne nodded.

"On your own?" she said.

It was out. It was like the table had fallen away and there was nothing to lean on.

"I'm sorry?" said her mother.

"Do you, like – do you live on your own?"

"No," said her mother. "No, I don't."

She was blushing.

"I was going to tell you other things first," she said.

"The good news, then the bad news," said Gráinne.

"No," said her mother. "Just – God."

She clutched her collar. She let go of it.

"Maybe I shouldn't have come," she said. "This isn't what I expected."

"What did you expect?" said Gráinne.

"I don't know," said her mother.

"You thought it would be easy."

"No," said her mother. "Not really. But, yes."

"Me too," said Gráinne. "I thought it wouldn't matter what you said, or anything."

Her mother nodded.

"I thought we'd have to just see each other," said Gráinne. "I've always thought that."

"How long?"

"Always," said Gráinne.

She watched her mother cry. She watched her wipe her eyes.

"I don't like the way you talk," said Gráinne.

She watched her mother.

"I don't think you're honest," said Gráinne. "I thought it would be different."

She gulped back. She knew she wouldn't cry.

"I thought it would make sense. When I saw you."

Her mother nodded. She wiped her eyes again.

"Will we start again?" she said.

"That's not honest either," said Gráinne. "It's just crap."

She stood up. She took her bag off the floor. She walked out.

She walked down the street. She didn't look back. She didn't hear anything. She walked to the bus stop. She waited. It was cold. Her mother hadn't followed her.

She got on the bus. She went home.

Her dad was at work. She went up to her room. She shut the door. She put on her headphones.

She wouldn't hear the bell. She wouldn't hear the phone.

CHAPTER SEVEN

It was dark now. It seemed like ages since they'd left, even a different day. But it hadn't been very long. It just felt like that. The boys were tired, even though they'd done nothing. The fresh air did it; that was what their mother said. They'd been gulping down the freshest air they'd ever tasted. They couldn't stop yawning.

They went along the tracks they'd made that morning. The tracks were hardened, and icy. It was getting even colder.

The dogs hadn't slowed a bit. They were still flying, little steps. Ears up, and tails in the air. One of the dogs had pooed while he ran. His bum was near the ground but he kept moving his legs, as if he had trousers that were down around his ankles. They laughed and nudged each other for ages after that. It was the funniest thing they'd ever seen, even funnier than the time their dad had leaned against the car door, and the door opened, and he fell out. The car was parked; he fell on to the grass.

They were glad to see the lights, and the hotel behind the lights. They were hungry. Tom thought, for the first time in his life, *I want hot food*. It had to be hot. He touched his nose. He couldn't really feel it.

He yawned again.

And Johnny yawned.

And Tom yawned.

The dogs brought them through the gate. The ice and snow were thinner here. The sled was shuddering. The runners screeched across the ice.

"Agon-ee," said Johnny.

Tom yawned.

Kalle didn't shout or make any kind of noise, but the dogs all stopped together. It was suddenly very quiet. The wind sound was gone, and the branches, and the dogs' feet on the snow, and their breath.

It was like an end. The day was over.

But it wasn't.

Kalle pulled them out of the sled. They were in the air and laughing before they really knew it. He put them down.

"Look – after – dogs," he said.

Tom loved the way he said that. They were in charge; they'd know what to do. He wasn't tired now. The boys released the dogs from their straps. Tom could feel the energy and life under their fur. And the energy seemed to run through his hands and arms. He took off his gloves. He loved the feel of the dogs. He could hear Aki's snowmobile. He could hear the other dogs. He looked, and saw their mother. She waved, and he got back to work. Holding the dogs, feeling their heartbeats and breath – Tom wasn't tired at all. He couldn't wait until the next day.

It was quieter now. Aki had turned off the engine. Very few people were talking. The dogs were getting raw meat for dinner, but Tom and Johnny didn't have to touch it. They were in charge of the water. The smell of the meat was disgusting. They could smell it in the dogs' breath when they bent down to pick up the water bowls. But it was funny. They pretended they were going to be sick.

"Are you coming, lads?" said their mother.

She was passing them, on her way back to the hotel with the other adults. They were all walking slowly and stiffly, like giant toddlers with full nappies. They held their backs; they rubbed their hands. But there was excitement in their eyes. They felt the same way Johnny did. They'd had one of the most brilliant days of their lives.

"In a minute," Johnny shouted to his mother.

"OK."

She followed the other adults. The man and woman from Belgium waited for her.

They heard her call back to them.

"Come in when Aki and Kalle tell you to."

They heard her again.

"OK?"

"OK," they shouted back.

Johnny didn't want to give up yet. He was hungry and very thirsty. He was kind of soggy and cold, but he wanted to stay with the dogs for a bit longer. They were better than any dogs he'd known. He'd never known dogs that were so friendly and so beautiful, so near to talking back to them.

Tom went to every dog, and every dog gave him the paw. Johnny was right behind him, and the dogs gave him the paw. They went around again; they laughed and ran. They nearly fell in frozen and not-so-frozen poo. They started whacking each other on the back. The big thumps filled the air around them. The dogs were getting excited. They began to jump at Johnny and Tom as they ran past.

Then Kalle's voice swallowed all other sound.

"Stop!"

They stopped.

And the dogs stopped.

And everything else stopped. Aki stopped walking. The other dog handlers stopped dropping raw meat into the dogs' dishes.

Kalle stared at Johnny and Tom.

"Sorry," said Tom.

"Husky – dogs – must – rest," said Kalle.

"OK," said Johnny.

They could hear the dogs panting, like they were agreeing with Kalle.

Kalle pointed at a bowl.

"Water."

"OK," said Tom.

"OK," said Johnny.

They brought the bowls to a big barrel full of water. The bowls were wooden, so the dogs' tongues wouldn't get stuck to the sides. They saw the ice on top of the water. They dipped the bowls in, and carried them back to each kennel. They filled every bowl. Tom's hands were freezing, but he didn't care. He brought the bowls to the dogs. Their names were on the kennels, above the entrances. Rock, the lead dog, Bruno, Hupö, Pomp. He patted every dog. The dogs looked up at him with their amazing eyes. Johnny gathered all the harnesses and hung them where Kalle showed him to. He straightened out the straps and halters.

They worked with Kalle for at least another hour. Their hands were sore, even with their gloves back on. They didn't care. They were nearly crying, their hands were so cold, and stiff. But, really, they didn't care. They loved the dogs. They didn't want to leave them.

But they did leave. There was nothing left to do. The dogs needed rest. Kalle was going home. They wondered what Kalle's house was like.

"Like Hagrid's," said Johnny. "In *Harry Potter*."

"Yeah," said Tom. "And full of dog stuff."

"Yeah," said Johnny. "And skulls – wolf skulls, and bear skulls, and dog skulls, and little bird ones on the mantelpiece."

"And all skins and stuff on the wall," said Tom.

"Yeah," said Johnny.

They walked across to the hotel. They crunched through some really good snow, but they never thought of stopping and making snowballs.

Johnny was hungry. He was tired. And there was something else. He felt different. He felt bigger. He'd been working, and he felt like a man.

"Wonder what's for dinner," said Tom.

"Yeah," said Johnny. "I hope there's chips."

"Yeah," said Tom.

He pushed the door. He felt the heat whack his face. He took off his gloves. He took off his hat.

They took off their boots. Their socks were still dry. They walked slowly to their room.

The Bedroom

She sat on the bed with her back against the wall. She cut pictures from magazines. From *Kerrang!*, the *NME*, and *Girl Metal*. The bed and her legs were covered with pieces of paper. The pictures she wanted to keep, she had in a pile on her thigh. She would put them up on her wall. Her father had asked her not to use Blu-tack, because it took off the paint and plaster. But she didn't care. She put up new pictures to cover where the paint was gone. And, anyway, it was her wall. It was her room.

He was good that way, her father. He always knocked. He never just came in. He never had, even when she was small. Not since the night she told him that she wanted to go to sleep with the door closed. She remembered that.

Eight years ago.

It was her room.

But it wasn't. Nothing here was hers. She didn't

belong here. And now she knew – she was certain of it; it was a feeling, like being cold – she didn't belong anywhere.

It was dark outside. She was the only one in the house. Her mobile phone was off, deep inside her bag. Her father thought she was with her mother. The others were in Finland, or wherever – somewhere stupid with snow.

She had her headphones on. Punk was the best. It was angry. It was funny. It was honest. And most of them were dead. Like most of the Ramones. And Joe Strummer and Sid Vicious. They were dead too.

She cut out a small picture of Joe Strummer. It was exactly like twenty pictures of Joe Strummer already on the wall, behind her head. She'd stick it up with the others and go over his face with a highlighter marker – yellow, or pink, or light blue, or even red. She'd already done it with different pictures of Marilyn Manson. The pictures of Joe Strummer were beginning to look like one big picture. Exactly what Gráinne wanted. Work in progress. That was what her art teacher had called whatever picture they were doing but hadn't finished. Gráinne had liked that. Work in progress. She'd liked the art teacher as well – the only one she'd liked.

She knew she was alone. The headphones were on, and she couldn't hear anything else. But she knew. She felt it in the wall. The front door being slammed, even being quietly closed; footsteps in the hall, someone coming up the stairs. When Gráinne was leaning against the wall, she'd feel it all in her back. The house moved when anyone moved. She could tell who it was, one of her brothers, or her father, her stepmother. She knew the way they moved, how heavy they were. The vibrations worked their way up the wall, to her back.

She was alone.

The way she liked it.

But she didn't. She didn't like it.

Sometimes, it was cool. When the rest of them were at work and school, she didn't feel left out or invisible. And later, when they all came home, she'd always sit on the bed and feel the house vibrate. Her back felt the movements – the messages. They were all watching telly; one of them was in the kitchen; her brothers were crawling up the stairs. Gráinne could read the house, even when the music was loud enough to hurt.

She could feel the cold pressing against the bedroom window, to the right of her face. She was alone. It was how she always felt. But it was different this time.

The future had been her mother. The things Gráinne had thought of; the things she'd dreamed, happening in New York, or even here in Dublin – they were all going to be with her mother. That was how

Gráinne had made it, for years, ever since she'd known she had a mother who was somewhere else. Waiting. Then her father had told her that her mother was coming home, and Gráinne had started to make the things really precise. Where they'd live in New York; how they'd live; why they'd laugh; what they were going to say to make sense of the years in between. They'd drink wine. Gráinne didn't really like it, but she'd sip. They wouldn't go for walks. Her mother would know that walks were stupid, even walks in Central Park, or on Rockaway Beach. The Ramones had a song called "Rockaway Beach". She'd play it for her mother, and she wouldn't look embarrassed. Gráinne wouldn't wear headphones. She'd be at home there. She'd fit in.

But it wasn't going to be like that. It wasn't going to be anything.

She didn't like her mother. Just that. She didn't even hate her.

She hated her father – but she liked him. She liked feeling his steps through the wall. She liked remembering when she was smaller and holding his hand; sometimes, she still felt it. She liked that he was always the same, that she could throw things and scream and get drunk and be brought home in a police car, and he'd always look the same way at her, and he'd always want to hold her hand. She liked hearing his car, knowing he was home. Knowing she could hurt him, and he wouldn't hurt her back. He was an idiot. But that wasn't his fault. Because – Gráinne knew this – the only adults who made real sense were dead.

The wall was still. There weren't even any cars or trucks going past. There were no neighbours slamming doors, no kids hitting balls against the front gates of their stupid houses. There was nothing. It was like her bed was the only thing in the world. She was a bit frightened now. She was too alone. She thought about taking the headphones off. But she wouldn't.

She didn't want to feel her mother in the wall. She didn't ever want to feel her steps, or hear her climb the stairs.

Her eyes were closed. She was alone. There was no one and nothing. Only Gráinne.

She opened her eyes.

Her father was there. Standing in front of her. The bedroom door was open, behind him.

She'd felt nothing in the wall. Maybe she'd been asleep. But she hadn't. The Ramones were still playing; there'd been no break in the song. But it was like waking up. She should have felt his car, his key in the front door, his big feet on the stairs. And her own door – it was open behind him.

He looked worried.

She took off her headphones.

He saw her looking at the door.

"I knocked," he said.

She said nothing. The wall had never let her down before. Everything was going wrong.

"You didn't answer," said her father. "I wasn't sure you'd be here."

"Well, I am," said Gráinne.

"I was worried," he said.

She picked up the headphones.

"Can I sit down?" he said.

"No," she said.

He smiled.

"What's so funny?" she said.

"It's kind of reassuring," he said.

"What is?"

"Your rudeness," he said. "I'd have been more worried if you'd said yes."

She said nothing. He stood there, looking – she knew the word – indecisive. He couldn't make his mind up. He didn't know whether to go or stay, say something or not. It was always the same. She liked the idea of him. But she hated it when he was there, like he was now. He'd told her once that he'd been into the Sex Pistols. That was a joke. And he'd told her that he'd seen The Clash, in 1982. But she hadn't believed him, and she hadn't asked him about it. There was no way.

"It's freezing in here," he said.

He leaned over and felt the radiator. He looked at the dial.

"It's on," he said. "But it's cold. It needs bleeding."

She didn't ask him what that meant. She didn't want to hear him explaining how the radiator worked.

"Why didn't you tell me?" he said.

She sighed.

"Tell you what?" she said.

"That was the radiator wasn't working."

She shrugged.

"Didn't notice," she said.

He sat down – on the chair at her old desk.

"Your granny phoned me," he said.

He meant her mother's mother; she knew that.

"She told me," he said. "A bit."

She stared at him, and away.

"I'm sorry," he said.

"What?"

"Ah look," he said. "I'm sorry it isn't working with your mother. I don't know how to express it properly. But I'm sorry."

"I don't need your sympathy," she said.

She wondered why she'd said that.

"Well," he said. "I'm just saying. And I mean it. I'd love it to go well for you."

"Did you talk to her?"

"Your mother?"

"Yeah."

"No," he said. "No. I didn't. She wants to come over."

"Here?"

"Yes."

"Now?"

"Ish. Whenever. But, yeah. Tonight."

He was looking straight at her.

"I can get out of your way," he said.

"No."

"No, which?"

"I don't want her to come here," said Gráinne.

"All right," he said.

He didn't move.

"Can I say something?" he said.

He waited. She shrugged.

"It's a free country," she said.

He smiled – then stopped. She hadn't seen him like this before; she didn't think she had. He didn't look uncomfortable, or like he wanted to get away. But it reminded her of something.

"Give her more time," he said.

"What about you?" said Gráinne.

"She's your mother," he said. "I was only her husband."

He smiled.

"I'm happy," he said.

"So am I," said Gráinne.

He'd caught her out; he didn't disagree with her. He was still looking straight at her.

"But I bet she isn't," he said.

"What?"

"Happy."

"That's her problem," said Gráinne.

"That's right," he said. "But it would probably be nice if she was."

"Happy?"

"Yeah."

She shrugged. She looked away.

He didn't move. He was letting her think. And she knew now what it reminded her of – or, *who* he reminded her of. He reminded her of her father, the way he used to be. The man who'd held her hand.

He stood up.

He sat down again.

"Can I say something else?" he said. "D'you mind?"

She shrugged again. It annoyed her. She hadn't meant to do that.

"Is that a yes?" he said.

He wasn't being sarcastic.

She nodded.

"Well," he said. "I love you."

He stood up.

"OK?"

She nodded.

"That never, ever changes," he said. "OK?"

She nodded.

"Will you talk to her tomorrow?" he said.

She looked at him. She nodded.

"Grand," he said. "I'll tell your granny. She'll be delighted. Is the morning OK for you, not too early? Or the afternoon."

"Afternoon," she said.

"Grand."

He went to the door.

"I'll leave you to it," he said. "They're having a great time, by the way."

She looked at him.

"The boys and Sandra," he said. "They phoned me earlier. They're having a great time."

"Big deal," said Gráinne.

CHAPTER EIGHT

They were on a lake again, but it wasn't the same lake as before. It was a different lake.

But it wasn't. Johnny could see that now. He saw the wooden house he'd seen the day before, the one that looked like it came from a story. He saw the house, and he suddenly knew the lake.

The day before. That was only yesterday, but it seemed much longer, even weeks ago. He'd slept for ten hours. His mother had had to wake him. She'd kept at him, and Tom.

"Come on, boys. Up, lads!"

He'd kept his eyes shut. It was too hard to open them, even though he knew she'd probably tickle him. But she didn't. She went away. He heard the door being closed softly. He must have slept again; he must have. The next thing he knew, there was something on his lip, right under his nose. Something warm, and wet, and smelly. And then something warm dribbled into his nose. He sat up. It was a rasher, a slice of bacon. His mother had put one under his nose.

"I knew that would wake you," she said.

"Breakfast in bed," said Johnny.

And he ate it.

Yesterday felt like weeks ago.

Yesterday they'd gone past the story house. Now, the house was straight ahead, right in front of them. The dogs had dragged them on to the same lake, but from a different place. Johnny and Tom both felt the same way; they were getting to know the wilderness.

"Wilder-ness!"

"Wilder-nesssss!"

It still sounded great, their voices spreading out, filling the world.

This was the real safari. Last night Johnny had slept in the hotel. Tonight he wouldn't. He'd be going further, and further. Further north, and further into the forest.

"Wilder-ness!"

In the brochure it was called a hut. That was where they were going. They were going deep into the forest, until it was too dark. Then they'd be staying in the hut. They'd be staying all night. There was no electricity and no hot water. It was made of wood and nothing else.

It was cold. It was starting to snow. The flakes whacked Tom's face. The sled was going fast, and the snow was getting thicker very quickly. He heard the hiss of the other sleds behind him, the runners going over the ice. His mother was on one of them. He hadn't seen her in a while. They'd had the morning break, the coffee and apple juice, about an hour ago. It was midday now, as bright and silvery as it would get. The snow was pouring down, sheets of white. It was covering the blanket that covered them. Tom pushed the snow off, and there was more snow there before he'd finished.

He heard Aki's snowmobile. He saw the headlights on the snow, two triangles that got bigger and sharper as the snowmobile came nearer.

Tom leaned out and looked behind. Just for a second – it was kind of scary.

Aki was side by side with Kalle. They shouted to each other, Aki first, then Kalle, then Aki again. They spoke in Finnish, but Tom and Johnny could tell; they were deciding what to do, maybe which way to go. They'd done it a couple of times before. Then Aki turned the snowmobile. He swerved away from their sled, on to the lake, and Tom watched as he kept turning and drove back to the other sleds behind them.

The snow wasn't as thick now. They didn't have to rub it off their faces. They watched the dogs. They loved watching the dogs. The way they trotted along, the way they seemed so happy. Eight dogs, in two rows of four. It looked so easy, and yet it was amazing. Tom couldn't imagine other dogs doing this. All dogs had a special skill. There were runners, or hunters, or pointers; they could all do one great thing. Their mother had told them that if they ever found a dog that cooked the dinner, they could keep it.

Tom turned a bit, so he could see Johnny better.

"Will we get a dog this Christmas?" he said.

The snow was getting heavy again. They were still going over the lake.

"Yeah," said Johnny.

"Between us."

"Yeah."

"A husky," said Tom.

"Yeah."

"Can you get huskies in Ireland?"

"Don't know," said Johnny. "I'd say so."

"Yeah."

Tom sat back again. Then he sat up again.

"He could pull us on my skateboard," he said.

"Cool," said Johnny.

He rubbed the snow off his face.

"To school even," said Tom.

"Yeah."

They laughed. They saw themselves, charging into the schoolyard behind their husky.

Then the dogs were changing direction. They were turning, towards the far bank. The snow was thick and fat again, like someone above them was dropping it off a shovel. Tom could hardly see Rock, the leader, and Hupö, at the front. He looked up, and back, at Kalle.

He nudged Johnny.

"Look."

"What?" said Johnny.

He looked, and saw. Kalle was wearing his hat.

"That means it's minus thirty," said Tom.

"Cool," said Johnny.

He didn't feel any colder. He was very cold already.

The trees got closer. They saw the gap. They saw, and felt, the dogs run off the ice, and up on to solid ground, then snow. The lake was gone, and so was the falling snow. They were in the trees. It was darker, but they could still see better because they didn't have snow in their eyes. It was quieter too, and it didn't seem as cold. Aki was behind them, somewhere. Johnny saw the snowmobile lights break the dark in front of them. It was scary and great. The lights jumped and turned, and went and came back, as the snowmobile went over humps and around the corners made by the trees. And when they came out of the trees the snow battered them – they laughed.

"Agon-eee!'

The dogs never slowed, not even when Pomp did another poo. His bum was just off the snow, and it looked like the other dogs were laughing as the harness held him up.

The sled went over the poo.

"Yeuk!"

The snow was really thick, on the ground and in the air. And the dogs finally slowed down. They were like dogs the boys had seen in the water, swimming, fetching sticks and balls in the sea at Dollymount, near where they lived. The huskies' backs went up and down in the same way, like they were bounding through the waves.

Johnny felt the sled shift suddenly. He looked behind, and Kalle was in the snow. He was pushing the sled, and the snow was over his knees. But they were still moving. And, soon – it took only a few pushes from Kalle – they were going properly again, back in among the trees, where the snow wasn't as deep and the dogs were back to normal.

But then they slowed down again.

Tom looked, and saw a sled beside them, empty, no one on it. Someone behind them had fallen off.

"I wonder was it Mam."

"Hope so."

"Hope not."

"So."

"Not."

"Eejit."

"Not."

Kalle stood on the brake, and they stopped, and it felt weird because they weren't moving. The silence filled their ears. They heard the other dogs behind them, and Aki's snowmobile. The light went over their heads and lit the trees and made them disappear, and then lit them again.

Kalle held the dogs from the other sled. The snowmobile was close now. Aki stopped, and the boys saw someone climb off it, behind Aki. It wasn't their mother. It was the man from Belgium. They knew his hat – it had a smiling deer on it – and his glasses were covered in snow and ice. He took them off and tried to wipe them clean. He smiled at the boys.

"Did you fall off?" said Tom.

"No," said the man. "The sleigh did not move in the snow."

He looked down at the snow.

"I removed my feet from the brake."

He lifted his boots, one at a time, to show them what he'd done. He grinned.

"And the sleigh was there no longer."

Kalle was waiting for the man from Belgium. Kalle's hat was skinny yellow and red stripes, with a floppy point at the top and flaps for over his ears. He hadn't tied the earflaps. The strings dangled on his snowy shoulders.

They heard Aki.

"And so! We go!"

The man from Belgium stood on the brake of his sled, and Kalle got back behind the boys. They could see all the other sleds behind them.

They heard their mother.

"All right, lads?"

"Yeah!"

"Bored yet?"

"No!"

"Not nearly!"

Kalle lifted his feet off the brake. And they felt it, from the front of the sled to the back; they heard the groan of the wood, as the dogs realized they were free to go. They were moving again. But they weren't as fast as usual. They had to bound through the snow. Then they were moving properly, and Aki's lights were far behind them.

It was dark. It was night now, even though it would have still been daylight in Dublin. It was much colder. Tom couldn't see clearly – he could hardly see anything. There were trees suddenly there, then gone. The sled jumped, went over a buried rock. But Tom couldn't really see. He began to wish they were at the hut.

The dogs ran out of the trees, into a clearing, and that was good because the boys could see a bit ahead, and the jumps and swerves made sense. But the snow was falling heavily again, and they had to keep getting it out of their eyes.

They heard Kalle behind them.

"Not – far."

He didn't shout but they heard him clearly. It was

windy now and, right beside them, near enough to touch, Johnny could see solid waves of snow. And he could feel the waves now too, because the dogs were going over them.

It was even darker now. There was no silver left in the air. They couldn't see anything ahead of them. There were no tree outlines, and no moon or stars, or anything else that would help them know where they were. Tom was glad they were squashed together, under the rug. They had Kalle too, behind them. He'd done this millions of times, and the dogs were his and they did everything for him.

But Tom was scared – a bit. He couldn't even see the snow falling on his face. He could only feel it. But he knew too, that this was great. This was something that might not ever happen again. It was absolutely amazing.

The boys tried to stay on the sled; they leaned back as far as they could. It wasn't the speed; it wasn't the swerves and jumps. It was the fact that they couldn't see. The dogs seemed even faster in the dark, and the speed seemed dangerous. But the quicker they went, the sooner they'd get to the hut. They could laugh then, and say it had been great. And it wouldn't be a lie, because it was great. Tom still thought that; he felt it. Kalle was behind them. They were charging into blackness, but they were safe.

Then they were flying – the sled was gone from

under them. The dogs were near. Tom heard them, and he saw a dark line – he thought it was one of the sled's runners – very close to his eyes. And he hit the snow. His face, his chin, his stomach – his breath was gone. His face was in the snow.

He got up quickly. He wasn't hurt; he wasn't sore. He didn't stand yet. He knelt in the snow and tried to see around him.

Johnny wasn't hurt either. He'd landed close to a tree, and there were rocks jutting around the trunk. He could see the rocks because the snowmobile was approaching and the lights came across the snow, like a fast, slithering animal. They lit the rocks, shining black and green. He turned, and saw Tom kneeling, his back to the lights. The sled was on its side. The blanket was on the snow, humped, like there was a body or something else quite big beneath it. He watched Kalle stand up slowly. Kalle picked up the blanket and shook it. He picked up the sled and put it back on its runners. The sled looked fine. Johnny could see nothing broken or damaged.

Tom watched the sled lifted out of the snow. He saw Kalle's hand, and then he saw the rest of Kalle. The lights from the snowmobile sprayed across everything, and Tom saw something that made him laugh.

"You are OK?"

It was Aki who spoke. He was walking up to Tom.

He'd left the engine running, so they could all see what was happening.

"Yeah," said Tom. "That was cool."

"And Johnny? You?" said Aki.

"I'm grand," said Johnny.

He stood up. His boots were deep in the snow. He looked across the sled at Tom.

"What are you laughing for?" he said.

"Look," said Tom.

He pointed.

"What?" said Johnny.

"Look at Rock," said Tom.

Johnny looked, and saw what Tom was laughing at. The dog was standing quietly, with Kalle's hat in his mouth. He laughed, and watched Rock wag his tail.

"He knows it's Kalle's hat," he said.

"Kalle's smell," said Aki. "His scent."

Kalle walked across to Rock and took the hat. He put it back on his head.

"You are cold, Kalle?" said Aki.

"Yes," said Kalle.

"Kalle is cold; it must be cold," said Aki.

"I'm cold," said Tom.

"It must be very cold," said Aki.

Kalle shook the blanket again. He tilted the sled, to get the snow off it. He shook it, then he let it drop.

"And so," said Aki. "Again we go."

He walked back to the snowmobile.

"How far?" they heard a voice.

It was a man, but the boys couldn't tell which one. They couldn't see him, behind the snowmobile lights.

"Five minutes," said Aki. "Maybe ten minutes."

"Not – far," said Kalle, as Tom and Johnny climbed back on to the sled.

They heard their mother.

"All right, lads?"

They couldn't see her.

"Yeah!" said Johnny.

"Yeah!" said Tom.

"Miss me?"

"No!"

"Ah, go on. You do!"

Tom and Johnny didn't answer. Kalle gently dropped the blanket over them.

"Not – very – wet," he said.

He tucked it under them. Then he walked around to the back of the sled.

"I wonder is he annoyed," Johnny whispered.

"Why?" said Tom.

"'Cos he fell off his own sled," said Johnny.

"Oh, yeah," said Tom, and he laughed again.

They heard a dog behind them howl. It was Hastro, their mother's dog, the one with the mad blue and brown eyes, who wanted to be the lead dog.

"Hurry up there, Kalle!" they heard their mother. "This fella's going crackers."

The boys laughed. And the sled was groaning, and moving again, slowly. The snowmobile lights were with them for a while, and they could see in front of them, the trees and the path through them, and Kalle's huge shadow, and even the point of Kalle's hat.

Then they picked up speed. Or maybe it just seemed like that, because they left the lights behind and charged straight into the black darkness again. They felt the sled climb the drifts. It tilted and swerved. They leaned back when they thought they were going to fall out. The rug came off, but Johnny grabbed it back before it went under the sled.

They saw the light.

Ahead of them – gone, then back. Between the trees. A red light.

"Is that the hut?" said Johnny.

"Yeah; must be."

"Is that the hut?" Johnny asked Kalle.

"Yes," said Kalle.

They'd made it. They were there.

The light stayed small, and disappeared. The sled turned. They could see a clear path. It was nearly a tunnel between the walls of snow-fat trees. The light was straight ahead. And they could see the shape of the hut.

"It's big," said Tom.

He wasn't disappointed. It was like a house. The roof was a big triangle, and he liked that. He'd imagined a shed, or a tent made of animal skins. But this was better. The dogs brought them closer, and he could see the windows. There was flickering light behind them – candles, or a fire. It would be warm in there already. Tom was freezing. They were closer now, and Tom could see inside. There was a lovely shining brown colour, and candle shadows ran across the wood.

The snow was hard here, and it wasn't thick. The sled was louder, going over ice.

There was a veranda at the front of the hut. Tom saw the icicles hanging from the roof. They were huge and amazing. One of them stretched down nearly as far as the wooden rail at the front of the veranda. He saw movement inside; he thought he saw a face. He could already feel the heat. He could nearly smell the food. He couldn't wait to take off his red suit. And his boots – his feet felt dead inside them.

The dogs stopped. The sled stopped. The boys got out of the sled. They rolled off. They let themselves fall on to the snow. They heard the other dogs behind them, and they could see Aki's lights through the trees. Like the night before, they'd have to help before their day was over. And, like the night before, they didn't mind, once they were in among the dogs.

"I'm bursting," said Tom.

"Me too," said Johnny.

Kalle was near them.

"Hey, Kalle," said Johnny. "Where's the toilet?'"

Kalle pointed at a smaller wooden building. It was down a bit of a hill, so they slid and fell, and pushed each other. It was great to be moving again.

It was great to be safe.

They climbed the steps to the toilet door. Tom lifted the wooden latch and pulled the door open. There was light inside, but it was still quite dark – and warm. They felt the heat on their faces. There were three big candles lighting the place. There were toilet cubicles, two of them, to the left, and a sauna right in front of them. The coals were red and there was a bucket of water beside it, with a little ladle for the water. Johnny took off his gloves. He lowered the ladle into the water.

"Stop messing with it," said Tom.

"Why?" said Johnny.

"You'll get caught."

"Doing what?" said Johnny.

He lifted the ladle out of the bucket and poured the water on to the coals.

"Big crime," he said.

They heard the hiss and felt the heat. Tom went into one of the cubicles. As he was closing the door, he felt Johnny trying to shove it open.

"Privacy, please," said Tom.

He pushed, and locked the cubicle door. He heard Johnny, doing Kalle's voice.

"I'll – be – back."

And he heard him go into the cubicle beside him. It took ages to get out of the stupid red suit. It was like peeling metal off himself. He was bursting. It was one of those wooden toilets, just a hole in a plank. He shoved the suit down to his knees. He'd be able to go now. He opened the zip of his jeans. He looked up at the roof. He closed his eyes. He started to go.

He opened his eyes.

Johnny was looking down at him.

"Where's the fire?"

Tom thought he'd wee all over the place, because he was laughing so much. But he didn't. Johnny's face was gone. Tom could hear him next door, doing the same thing Tom had just been doing.

Tom pulled up his suit.

They heard Kalle, outside.

"Irish boys!"

"Oh-oh," said Tom.

"The giant will eat us if we don't hurry up," said Johnny.

They ran outside and skidded back, to the dogs and Kalle. The other people had arrived, or were arriving. The boys heard the dogs and the different languages.

They worked with Kalle. They unhitched the dogs, one by one. Kalle brought Rock. Tom brought Pomp. And Johnny brought Bruno. They followed Kalle to a place away from the path, with hooks screwed into the trees. Kalle tied their straps to the hooks. The snow was thick here, and some of the dogs went round and around, and made a hole for themselves. Then they lay down in the snow, with their noses tucked under their tails.

They brought all the dogs to this place. Then they followed Kalle across the deep snow, to a big water barrel at the corner of the hut. The top of the barrel was level with Johnny's chin, and Kalle had to bend down to whack the ice with his elbow. They heard the ice creak and break. Kalle wasn't wearing gloves now. And he took off his hat. He put it on the veranda rail. Then he picked up the big pieces of ice from the barrel with his bare hands and he threw them into the snow.

He stood back. He looked at Tom and Johnny.

"Good – workers," he said.

He didn't smile, but they knew he was being nice.

He walked away.

They knew what to do. There was a pile of wooden bowls on the veranda, under the rail. They dipped the bowls into the barrel. They had to lift their arms to reach, and the water ran down their sleeves. It was horrible, but they didn't mind it too much. They were working for the dogs.

They walked among the dogs, through the light that came from the hut. The other people had arrived. The rest of the dogs were being tied. Aki's lights sprayed across the snow and lit the dogs and the legs of the people in its way, and made crazy shadows that merged and broke. Then the snowmobile engine was off, and the light and shadows were gone.

They heard Aki.

"Home, sweet home."

The boys put water in front of all the dogs. They patted them all, especially the ones who'd pulled their sled. The dogs were tired; Tom could feel that through his gloves. It was like their blood had slowed down, and they were getting ready to sleep. They pushed their snouts against the boys' hands.

The boys were finished now; their work was done. They went up the steps to the veranda. They did what they saw the man from Belgium do, in front of them. They stamped their feet, to make the snow and ice drop off their boots. They followed the man from Belgium into the hut. They felt the warmth, like a thick invisible wave. They saw the man from Belgium take off his glasses; the lenses were covered in steam. They saw the other people, the woman from Belgium, and the others. They saw Aki.

They didn't see their mother.

The Kitchen

Gráinne watched her mother looking around the kitchen.

"This is strange," she said.

"No, it isn't," said Gráinne.

"Oh, dear," said her mother.

She sounded like the mothers of some of Gráinne's friends – from the time when Gráinne had friends. No matter what the mothers said – "Turn that down," "Is that all you're going to eat?" – the message had always seemed the same. The sad breath that came with the words, and the same half-closed eyes.

"Oh, dear, what?" said Gráinne.

They were sitting at the kitchen table. The table was between them. It was twenty past three. Gráinne saw that on the clock, on the wall above her mother's head. Her father was in the house, somewhere. He'd stayed home. He hadn't gone to work.

"I'll get out of your way," he'd said.

He'd smiled at Gráinne and walked out of the kitchen, leaving Gráinne with her mother.

It was the first time he'd seen her mother since she'd left. Gráinne thought of that now, for the first time. She was nearly certain it was true. Her mother had rung the bell. Her father had answered the door. They must have stood looking at each other. Gráinne didn't know for how long. She'd been upstairs, in her room. Not listening.

It was what Gráinne had wanted. She'd wanted him to stay.

"I can go somewhere else while she's with you. I can be gone when she arrives."

"No," Gráinne had said.

"No?"

"No."

"All right," he'd said. "I'll stay, if you want me to."

It must have been weird for him, seeing his wife – his ex-wife. She wondered – was he OK? He was probably in the front room. Maybe in his bedroom. She hadn't heard him going up the stairs. He was probably in the front room. Maybe looking out the window.

Her mother looked straight at her.

"Will I go now, Gráinne?" she said. "Or will we try?"

This was important. Gráinne knew. She had one chance. It was her choice.

She looked at her mother.

"Try," she said.

"Good."

They looked at each other. Her mother didn't smile. She knew too – everything was vital. Every word, every expression.

"I said it was strange," she said.

She lifted her hand. She waved it around.

"What I meant was, it was strange to be back. It hit me," she said. "I used to live here."

Gráinne said nothing.

"It hasn't changed much," said her mother.

It wasn't true. The room had changed a lot. Gráinne remembered it the old way. There was a different fridge, and the counter hadn't been there before, and other stuff. But it was the same room. So it must have been strange for her mother. Bad memories. And that made Gráinne angry. Why were her mother's memories bad? What had been so bad, enough to make her mother leave her? It was how Gráinne had felt for years, all her life: *What did I do? Why did you leave?*

"Why didn't he move?"

Her mother's voice surprised her.

"What?" said Gráinne.

"Your dad," said her mother. "Why didn't he move?"

"Move house?"

"Yes."

"I don't know," said Gráinne. "Why should he have?"

"I don't know," said her mother.

Because you did? Gráinne wanted to say. But she heard how it would sound; she heard it in her head. It wasn't the way she wanted to sound.

"We liked it here," she said.

It was true.

Her mother nodded.

The house had never been a bad place. And it wasn't just *he*. It was *we*. Gráinne wanted to say that too. But she didn't. *We liked it here*. That was enough. *We*.

Me.

"Of course," said her mother.

She smiled.

"I liked it too," she said. "Especially the garden."

Gráinne remembered helping her mother in the garden. She'd had her own tools. They were plastic, but they'd worked. She'd been able to dig little holes and cut twigs. She'd loved it, even on the days when it was cold. They'd come back in, for hot chocolate. They'd sit at the table, here, and drink together. *One, two, three*. They'd pick up the cups at the same time, and sip, and put them down so their cups tapped the table at the exact same time.

Her mother was looking out the window. She'd lifted herself a bit off her chair. She sat down again, properly.

"It looks good," she said.

It didn't; not really. Her dad wasn't interested. He

cut the grass when it got too long for her brothers to play football. And Sandra, her stepmother – Gráinne remembered her stepmother looking out the window. She looked at the rain and said, "If that garden had a roof it would be lovely."

Her mother put her arms on the table.

"I wish it was easy," she said.

She looked straight at Gráinne.

"I wish I could just say a few things and make it all OK," she said. "It would be lovely."

Gráinne nodded, once. She didn't think she understood; she wasn't sure. But she was listening. That was what the nod was for.

She made herself look at her mother.

"You probably," her mother began, then stopped. She lifted her hands, and put them down again.

"I've no right to say what you probably think or don't think," she said. "But –"

She smiled, and sighed.

"You probably want to know why I left."

Gráinne didn't nod. She tried not to move.

"I had to," said her mother. "That's all I can say. I had to."

"Why?" said Gráinne.

Her voice surprised her. She sounded calm.

"That's where it's hard," said her mother. "It's where words don't work. I can't give you a neat answer. Will I go on?"

"Yes."

"So," said her mother. "OK. It had nothing to do with your dad. With Frank. Not really. He's a lovely man. I thought that when I was leaving."

Gráinne heard the gulp. Her mother was crying.

"It's so good to be able to talk to you like this," she said.

She pointed at her eyes, before she wiped them.

"It's relief," she said. "That's why I'm crying. Will I go on?"

Gráinne nodded.

"Thank you," said her mother. "It had nothing to do with you, Gráinne. That might sound stupid, or strange. Even horrible. But it didn't. I loved you. I *love* you."

Everything in Gráinne told her to get up now and go. She thought she'd explode or die. *Push back the table. Smash it into her chest. Scream till it's all gone.* She wanted to go before she had to hear anything else.

But she stayed still. She made herself breathe in. She said nothing. She looked at her mother. She made herself do it. She wanted to scream.

"Will I go on?" said her mother.

She wanted to scream, spit, grab her mother's hair, and her own hair, and pull.

But she nodded.

And something happened inside her. When she

nodded, it was like she'd stepped into a new place. She'd left something behind. She wasn't sure; something had happened.

"I just knew," said her mother. "I had to go. I was so unhappy and confused. I was going to die. I'm not exaggerating. I still think that, looking back at it – here. I was going mad. Something in me."

She stopped. She looked straight at Gráinne. And Gráinne knew. She'd nod, and her mother would talk.

She nodded.

"You get married," said her mother. "You have children – a child. You turn from one person into another person."

And now – just now – Gráinne understood her mother. Because that was how Gráinne felt. She'd just turned into another person. That was what had just happened to her, when she'd nodded a minute ago, and let her mother talk.

"I don't think it happens to men," said her mother. "Not the same way. But I'm not sure. I never really talked to Frank about it. We couldn't. We just –"

She stopped. She looked at the window. It was starting to get dark.

"Anyway," she said. "I loved being your mother. I really loved it. That probably sounds – I don't know – awful. But it's true."

Gráinne nodded.

"And I loved Frank," said her mother. "But the old

me hadn't gone. And I felt like I was killing the old me and I didn't want to do that. Because it *was* me. And I didn't want to kill myself. And I would have. If I'd stayed."

She was crying again, a bit.

"Am I making sense?"

"Yes," said Gráinne.

"Really?"

"Yes."

"Will I go on?"

"Yes."

"Good," said her mother. "Thanks. I have to be honest here. I wasn't confused. I knew what I had to do – what I was doing. And that was what I did. I went. So –"

She wasn't crying now. She wasn't pleading. She wasn't asking Gráinne to forgive her. She was treating Gráinne like an equal. And Gráinne had made it happen. By nodding every time her mother asked, by letting her mother speak, Gráinne had decided that this was going to happen.

CHAPTER NINE

Their mother wasn't there. The boys saw that quickly. She wasn't in the big room.

They could smell hot chocolate.

They looked behind them. She wasn't coming in. In fact – they both now thought of it – they hadn't seen her out there. Johnny went back to the door. He went out to the veranda. Tom followed him. They looked across the yard, and down the tree-lined path. There was no one out there, only the dogs.

They went back in. She might have been in a smaller room. She might have been behind all the other people.

But she wasn't there.

"She's hiding outside," said Johnny. "Having a smoke."

But everyone there was looking at them, and some of them were smiling, the way you smile at sick people.

"Where's our mam?" said Tom.

Aki stepped forward. He was putting on his crash helmet. Kalle was behind him, zipping up his jacket.

"Your mother—" said Aki.

"Where is she?" said Tom.

"She fell, I guess," said Aki.

"Where is she?" said Tom, again.

Aki pointed at the window.

"Back," he said. "Not far."

"Where?"

Tom felt a fist, growing bigger inside him. Quickly bigger, in his stomach. It hurt.

Johnny saw the other people whispering, passing on the information. *She's missing. She's missing.* He saw huge flakes of snow begin to hit the window, and slide down, on to more snow.

"It is cool," said Aki. "She will be found. You want hot chocolate?"

Tom couldn't answer. The big fist was charging up his throat. He was going to be sick; he thought he was.

But Aki and Kalle were in charge. They were at the door. And they didn't look worried and panicky.

"We will be back very soon," said Aki. "With your mother."

He rubbed his bum.

"I hope she did not fall so hard," he said.

Tom smiled. Johnny did too. They didn't want to be

more worried than Aki. It was the wilderness, but the boys had been through it, yesterday and today, and they'd gone over the same lake twice. It wasn't all that big. Aki and Kalle would find her.

Aki smiled, and followed Kalle. They were gone.

Johnny went to the door. Tom followed him. They watched Kalle hitch his dogs to the sled. They watched Aki walk to the far side of the yard, to the snowmobile. He climbed on, and turned it on. They watched him push it back a bit with his feet. Then he turned and slowly drove down the tree-lined path. Kalle followed him. They watched the two men turn a bend, first Aki, then Kalle. They watched Aki's headlights in the distant trees, until they couldn't see them any more, and they couldn't hear his engine.

"You want hot chocolate?"

They turned.

There was a woman at the door. They hadn't seen her before. She wore an apron with a reindeer on it, and yellow trousers.

"Yes," said Johnny.

He nudged Tom.

"He does too," he said.

Tom didn't feel too sick now. He knew that Aki and Kalle would be back soon. They were experts.

"Come," said the woman.

She stood away from the door, and the boys followed her into the hut. The other people were standing there, looking at the boys and smiling like mad. They'd all taken off their red suits, and their boots were in a line along the wall nearest the door.

The new woman walked to the big table. The people stood back to make room for her, and they stood back even further when Johnny and Tom followed her.

"You will take off your suits, perhaps," said the man from Belgium.

The boys didn't answer. They weren't going to take their suits off. They weren't going to sit down. Not until they saw their mother.

The new woman turned to face the boys, and she was holding two mugs nearly as big as flowerpots.

"Come."

She was smiling. She was nice. She must have worked there, in the hut. She looked like she was in charge. She waited till Tom and Johnny had taken off their gloves, and then she gave them each a mug.

"Very hot, I think," said the man from Belgium.

"Very good," said someone else.

The boys stood beside the table and drank their hot chocolate.

"Good?" said the woman.

"Yes," said Johnny.

And Tom nodded.

"Your mother will be very cold, I think," said the man from Belgium.

The boys looked up at him. He was smiling, and everybody else was smiling.

"I will, for sure, make hot chocolate for the mother," said the new woman.

"Very good," said the man from Belgium.

The boys stood there. The other people spoke very quietly. Some of them sat. Johnny listened for Aki's engine. He looked at the window. He saw the snow land and slide on the glass. The glass was slowly being covered.

The boys felt hot now. They were standing near the fire. Tom was looking at it for a while before he noticed the fish. It was on a metal rack. The top of the rack was leaning on the wall inside the fireplace. The bottom part was resting on the floor. The fish was big. It was lying across the fire, just above the flames. It must have been a salmon, or something like a salmon. It was cooking very slowly. Tom began to smell it.

He hated fish.

Johnny moved. He jumped, like he'd been pinched or something.

"What?" said Tom.

He listened, but he couldn't hear anything outside.

"If she fell off the sleigh," said Johnny.

"What d'you mean?" said Tom.

"If she fell off," said Johnny.

"If?"

"That's what Aki said," said Johnny. "She fell off, yeah?"

"Yeah," said Tom.

"Well, if she did," said Johnny. "Why didn't the dogs come here, alone?"

"What?" said Tom.

"The dogs," said Johnny. "Like, when Mam fell off yesterday. Remember?"

"Yeah," said Tom.

They both spoke quietly.

"The dogs kept going," said Johnny. "Till they caught up with Kalle."

"And Rock," said Tom.

"Yeah."

They looked at each other.

"They didn't catch up this time," said Tom.

"No."

"Why not?"

Then they heard the engine. They heard it before anyone else. And Tom said the name they'd both been thinking.

"Hastro."

Hastro was the rogue dog, the tricky one their mother hadn't been able to hitch to her sled. Johnny knew what Tom meant – Hastro might have done something bad.

They moved to the door. Johnny got there first. Now the engine was quite loud. The other people saw the headlights brighten the snow in the window.

Johnny and Tom stopped on the veranda. They saw nothing except the headlights. They couldn't see behind the lights. They were pointed straight at them. Then Aki moved off the centre of the path, and they could see more. They saw Kalle's dogs, and the sled behind them. They could see Kalle now, standing big behind the sled.

And that was all.

The engine stopped. The sled went past the snowmobile. The dogs were panting. Johnny and Tom could see the sled. It was empty. Their mother wasn't there.

They saw Aki. They heard his boots on the snow. They saw Kalle behind him, unhitching the dogs.

They looked at Aki's face. He was coming up the steps.

He smiled.

"She fell off not so near, I guess," he said.

He was right in front of the boys. He held up a mobile phone.

"We will find her," he said.

"She doesn't have her mobile phone with her," said Johnny.

"The rescue people," said Aki. "I will call them."

The snow was thick. The flakes were huge and falling straight, like stones.

"Come," said Aki.

He put his hands on their shoulders and gently pushed them to the door, into the hut.

Tom felt numb. His face was cold; the rest of him was hot. He felt the shivers coming. He was going to be sick. The floor was swaying.

Johnny nudged him. Tom looked. He saw Johnny's face, and he knew – Johnny had a plan.

Kalle was behind them, coming in the door. He looked at the boys.

"Not – worry," he said.

They didn't answer. They were afraid to hear their voices.

Aki was talking quietly on his mobile. He spoke in Finnish, and he was looking at a map on the wall as he spoke. He stopped speaking and put the phone on the table. Kalle was beside him now. They both looked at the map.

The boys had seen a map exactly like it, back at the hotel. But they hadn't really been able to read it. It was all just brown, no towns or big names. It was what a map of the wilderness should look like. Tiny numbers, and a few tiny names.

The new woman came at the boys with more hot chocolate in big cups.

"There is more for your mother," she said, and she smiled.

Johnny took his cup.

"Thank you."

Tom took his; he copied Johnny.

"Thanks very much."

They didn't drink. They held the cups. They watched Kalle and Aki looking at the map and talking. All the other people stood around, behind them. The man from Belgium leaned forward and pointed at something on the map. They watched Kalle check his belt, the things on it, the compass, the knife. Aki went to the table and opened a white box. They saw a red cross on the lid. The men and women stood around and looked into the box as Aki checked that everything was there.

Johnny and Tom looked at the window and watched the snow cover the last bit of window glass. Their mother was out there, under the snow, and the snow was getting deeper and deeper.

"Come on," said Johnny; he only whispered.

They stepped backwards, very quietly, to the door; it hadn't been closed. They stepped out on to the veranda. Johnny bent down and put his cup on the boards. And Tom did the same.

"Come on," said Johnny.

They went down the steps. They ran across the snow. They didn't slide or skid.

They took Kalle's dogs. They were quick. They untied four of them and brought them over to the sleds. They kept looking over at the hut. The adults were still in there, being like adults – busy and nice, but kind of stupid.

They tied the dogs to two sleds, two dogs for each sled. They didn't have time to get the other four. Johnny thought the dogs would be strong enough to pull them.

The dogs were tied. They were ready to go.

It had been easy.

"I'll go on this one," said Johnny.

Rock, the leader, was at the front.

"OK," said Tom.

He didn't mind. It was Johnny's idea. He stood on the brake, at the back of the second sled.

"But how will you get Rock to go?" he said. "You're not Kalle."

"Easy," said Johnny.

He held up something. Tom couldn't see what it was. Then it was nearer, and Tom could see that it was Kalle's hat and that Johnny was holding it on the end of a long stick.

"Brilliant," said Tom.

"Ready?" said Johnny.

"Yeah," said Tom. "But hurry."

He could see people coming out on to the veranda. He felt bad, and a bit disloyal. He liked Kalle and Aki; he thought they were great. But everything in Tom – his brain, his blood, everything that made him Tom – everything told him that what he was doing was right.

He'd find his mother – him and Johnny – quicker than anyone else.

He saw Johnny hold out the stick with the hat stuck to it, over the dogs' backs and heads. He held the stick, so the hat was just in front of Rock's nose.

Rock sniffed. And he started to move. He pulled, to get at the hat. Johnny rested the stick against the handle of the sled. He was able to hold the sled and the stick with one hand.

Rock pulled. Bruno, beside him, pulled too. Tom watched Johnny's sled move slowly away, down the tree-lined path. He looked behind him, and felt his own sled move. Hupö and Pomp were pulling him.

People were running across the snow. Aki and Kalle. He heard shouts, but they boomed and made no sense.

Tom was moving.

Fast.

He turned forward, and saw Johnny turn a bend. Tom was right behind him, holding on to his sled. His feet were wide apart. His balance was good. It felt good, natural. They flew into the cold, and the cold stopped him from crying.

He was going to find his mother. They were going to find her. Him and Johnny. They were going to find her.

He looked behind. There was no sign of the hut, or lights. They were back in the wilderness.

He went over a bump. The sled was off the ground, and back. His feet stayed on the foot plates. He could feel his hands sweat in the gloves. He kept his eyes on Johnny.

Johnny's hand was already sore, the one holding the stick. But he didn't mind; he didn't let it matter. He had to concentrate on what was ahead. There was no light, and the trees were close. The snow was huge and heavy. He had to watch the dogs. He could tell what was coming by looking at their backs and ears. Their eyes were his. He'd learned this over the past two days, watching them as they pulled him across the land and ice.

They were going to find her. He knew it. The cold didn't matter. And the dark didn't matter. They were going to find her. He had to keep thinking that.

He looked behind him, quickly. Tom was there. He even waved.

Johnny wiped the snow off his face. The sled jumped before he got his hand back to the handle. He stayed on – it was easy. He held on to the stick. He had to push his palm down on it, to trap it between the handle and his hand. He had to use the weight of his wrist and arm to keep the stick in the air, above Rock's snout.

He listened. He couldn't hear the snowmobile. Just his dogs and Tom's dogs. Their breath, their steady pace.

They were going to find her. Johnny looked at the dogs' backs. They were straight, and the ears were up. They knew where they were going.

They were going to find her. Johnny could think that – he could feel it and know it – as long as they kept moving.

They charged through the dark. They went under high, thick trees. They felt them, right over their heads, and it was even darker. Tom could see nothing. He could hear the dogs, but he couldn't see them.

The Kitchen

It was dark now. It was cold. Gráinne heard the click, the central heating coming on. But it would be ages before the radiator was warm enough. She rubbed her arms.

She was at the window, looking at the light outside. The light moved as her mother moved. She was looking at the plants and flowers she'd planted there, years ago. She was trying to find them with a torch.

She'd seen the torch on top of one of the shelves.

"Oh, look."

It had seemed funny, when her mother decided to go out and look for her flowers in the dark. But she'd been gone too long, or something. It wasn't funny now.

Gráinne couldn't see her mother properly. The light was on in the kitchen, so the window was like a mirror. She could see herself and things behind her. She could have gone across to the switch and turned off the light. But she didn't want to do that. She wasn't sure why not. It would have looked too much like she was spying. Something like that; she wasn't sure. It just seemed better to leave the light on.

Then she thought: *She can see me*. She couldn't see her mother, but her mother could see Gráinne, at the window, staring out.

She sat down at the table. She shouldn't have stood there for so long. Like a little girl looking for her mammy.

She didn't like this. The good feeling was slipping away. The confidence she'd felt when she'd listened to her mother, when she'd known when to nod and listen. She didn't think that feeling was there now in her. She wished her mother would come back in, before it became too hard to start again.

She thought about looking for her father. But then her mother would come back in and think she had to go.

She felt stuck, between her mother and her father. One bad move would let one of them down. It wasn't fair. She hated the way she was always on trial. She could feel the anger now. She tried to remember the good feeling she'd had a few minutes before; she tried to feel it. But it was disappearing, and now she didn't want it. She wanted to be angry. It was something she could actually trust. Something she knew and recognized. She could feel it rising through her.

She heard steps on the path outside. Her mother was coming back in.

Gráinne tried to stop it. She rubbed her arms, hard. She tried to rub the anger away, like sand off her skin. The door opened. She felt the cold from outside slither around the kitchen. She rubbed her arms.

CHAPTER TEN

The trees weren't as thick here. Tom could see Johnny, just ahead of him. He could see the tracks of Johnny's sled. He could see his own dogs run along the tracks. He kept his knees bent. It was easier to stay on that way.

He looked back quickly, and saw the light. It was far behind them, among the trees, and gone, and there again.

He shouted.

"They're behind us."

He heard Johnny.

"OK."

They were still on the main path. Johnny could make out where the sleds and snowmobile tracks had flattened the snow. It was the way they'd come earlier, on their way to the hut.

"Where are we going?" Tom shouted.

"This way," Johnny shouted back.

"Where?" Tom shouted.

"Following Rock," Johnny shouted back.

That made sense. Rock was the leader. He'd know where they were, and where they were going.

But Rock followed Kalle. That was why they were moving now, through the darkness. Rock was running after Kalle's hat. Johnny had tricked him so easily. But that didn't worry Tom. It was one of the interesting and complicated things about people and dogs and how they lived together. The boys were following a dog that was stupid enough to think that the hat was Kalle, but the dog was a brilliant dog, and they were right to be following him.

The ground was still mostly flat. The trees were close again, on either side of the path, so the snow wasn't too bad, because the trees were like a roof. It was darker again, but Tom could see.

Johnny tried to see ahead, to see if he recognized anything they were passing. This might have been another path that other sleds and snowmobiles used all the time. He was flying into the dark, and really quickly. He just had the dogs' backs; they were the only things he had to navigate with. There were no stars. Anyway, he didn't know much about stars. His dad had started to explain it to him once, about the stars and how sailors could cross the oceans just by looking at them. But it had been boring, the way his dad had tried to tell him.

He hoped he'd see something soon. Something that could tell him how far they'd come. He rubbed more snow from his face. The stick with the hat shifted, but he didn't let it slide from under his hand. His hand hurt a bit, where he had to push down the stick. But it wasn't bad.

He looked behind. He adjusted his weight; he bent his left knee. He looked, and saw the lights that Tom had seen. The snowmobile. He wasn't worried. It wasn't a race. He wasn't afraid of being caught. If Aki caught up with them, fine. There'd be more people to find their mother. That was what it was about. It wasn't a game or adventure. They were going to find their mother.

He heard Tom.

"How far?"

He shouted back.

"Don't know."

Then he thought of something else. He shouted it.

"Are we there yet?"

He did it in the whiny voice that drove their dad mad when they were going anywhere in the car.

He heard Tom laugh. And Tom shouted back.

"Are we there yet?"

"Are we there yet?"

"Are we there yet?"

"Wil-derness!"

A huge rock went past Johnny's face. He saw it; then it was gone. He'd been moving, not the rock, but it felt like the rock had shot past him. He gripped the sled. He went over a bump, and ducked under a very low branch; he felt the snow on his shoulders.

Tom didn't know where he was; he hadn't a clue. There was nothing he thought he'd seen before. But he wasn't lost; it didn't feel like that. Because of the dogs. He would never have walked through darkness like this. Or cycled. Not for money, or anything. It wasn't the dark; he wasn't afraid of the dark. It was what was *in* the dark. What was waiting. Holes, rats, crooked fingers, teeth. Not seeing; not being able to see. That was what frightened him.

But he wasn't really frightened now. The dogs were with him and he was going to find his mother.

A branch shot out at him. It slashed his face. He could feel the sting. He thought he could feel the blood on his cheek. The trees were close; they were trying to grab him.

But he wasn't really scared.

He looked behind again. He held on extra tight; he tried to make his legs heavy. He couldn't see anything. Then a branch brushed his back. He heard it before he felt it – another tree trying to grab him. He turned back again, and looked straight ahead.

Tom liked Aki. And he really liked Kalle. But they'd let him down. That was how it felt. They'd gone off, and come back without his mother. But that wasn't it. He didn't blame them for that, even though it was their wilderness and they were supposed to know everything about it. But he didn't blame them. It was more about the feeling he'd had when he watched them getting ready to leave the hut the second time, when Kalle was checking his belt and Aki was checking the first-aid box. They should have been faster. And they should have looked worried. But they'd been more interested in not upsetting Tom and Johnny. They'd pretended that it wasn't really an emergency. They'd treated Tom and Johnny like kids. Tom and Johnny *were* kids. But that was where lots of adults got it wrong. Kids didn't need to be treated *like* kids, or how most adults thought kids were – stupid. *Your mother is missing. It is very dangerous. We must find her. Quickly.* That was what they should have said. Tom and Johnny would have agreed with them, because Tom and Johnny already knew it. But, instead, they'd smiled and offered them hot chocolate.

Tom could feel the hot chocolate in his stomach. It was sloshing around as the sled bounced and turned. He tried not to think of it.

The dogs were different. The dogs were honest. The dogs weren't looking around and thinking, *He's too young.* They weren't slowing down because he was only ten. The dogs were doing what they were supposed to do.

They'd find her.

Johnny lifted his arm, but it was too late. The

branch had already hit him. It felt like a screech, across the side of his face, just under his eye. It was black for a minute – he couldn't open his eyes. The pain was chopping at him. He put his hand back on the sled. And opened his eyes.

He could see.

But the pain was horrible. It was much stronger, sharper than the cold. It burst out of the cold. He closed his eyes. The pain was right above them.

He waited for it to fade.

The dogs kept going.

It was like the times he'd eaten ice cream too fast and got brain freeze. The worst pain ever, until it began to fade, and it became a joke. This pain started to fade, but it wasn't going to be a joke.

He opened his eyes again.

He knew where he was. It was the way the trees spread out, and the tops of the stones he could see jutting out of the snow, around the trunks of some of the trees. They'd been there earlier. It was where they'd fallen out of the sled, where Rock had picked up Kalle's cap.

Johnny lifted the stick, and the cap. He put his foot on the brake. The dogs stopped. Johnny looked around. It was definitely the same place.

Tom's dogs stopped.

"What?" said Tom.

"This is where we fell off," said Johnny.

"Is it?"

He looked around.

"Yeah," said Johnny.

"But Mam fell off after us," said Tom.

"Yeah," said Johnny.

Tom rubbed the snow from his face.

"So we should have passed her back there," he said.

He looked behind, where they'd just come from.

"Ages ago."

"I know," said Johnny.

"Will we go back?" said Tom.

They could hear Aki's engine. They could see the lights.

"No," said Johnny.

"Why not?" said Tom.

"She's not back there," said Johnny. "We didn't see her."

He pointed back, at Aki's light.

"And they haven't seen her either."

"Where is she?" said Tom.

It was hard saying the words; he was afraid he'd cry. He wasn't sure if Johnny had heard him. It took him ages to answer.

"Don't know," said Johnny. "But I bet I know what happened."

"What?"

"She didn't fall off," said Johnny.

"What happened then?" said Tom.

Aki's engine was getting nearer.

"Hastro did something," said Johnny.

"What?"

"He decided he was the leader, or something," said Johnny. "And he ran off, with Mam still on the sled."

Tom could see it in his head. The rogue dog waiting until Rock was far ahead, then making a break for it, pulling his mother's sled down a narrower path, away from Rock and Kalle, making the other dogs go with him. He could easily see it. But –

"Why didn't she jump off?" he said.

"Don't know," said Johnny. "Maybe she didn't know."

"Yeah."

"Maybe she just thought she was way behind every-one else."

They heard the engine. They saw the lights behind them, jumping along the trees.

"Will we wait for Aki and Kalle?" said Tom.

"No," said Johnny.

Tom would have liked the adults with him now. He knew they wouldn't be angry. But he knew that Johnny was right.

"Yeah," he said. "They'll just stop searching for Mam, because they'll think they've found us and that's enough. They'll bring us back to the hut first. And it'll have to start all over again."

"Yeah," said Johnny. "Let's go."

The pain wasn't bad now. There was no blood going

into his eyes. And it was much colder when they weren't moving. His arm ached as he held up the stick and hat, over Rock's snout. But it didn't matter.

The dogs began to move.

"Where will we go?" said Tom.

"Just follow the dogs," said Johnny.

Johnny was right, Tom thought. *Follow the dogs.* That was enough. Tom took his feet off the brake. And his dogs began to pull. They began to pick up speed.

The snow was falling thick. Johnny could feel more of it than he could see. He didn't mind. The flakes landed on his face, where the branch had hit him. It smothered the stinging feeling.

Then he couldn't feel as much snow on his face. They were in thick trees again. He could feel the branches brush his shoulders. He didn't like it. The dogs slowed, and speeded up, like they were fighting their way over snow that no sleds had gone over before. But he couldn't see much. It was the darkest yet.

Tom could hear the trees breathing – he was sure he could. And he could feel their fingers. The dogs were slow now, so it felt like the twigs and pine needles were pulling at Tom's sleeves and hat. The trees were close, and they were closing in. The path was getting narrower, and he wondered if it was a path at all. They'd soon be stuck under heavy branches and thorns. There were snakes in Finland. There were wolves; there were bears.

Needles swiped his face. He cried out – he thought he did. He wasn't sure. He tried not to – the needles did it again, across his face, like a prickly cloth. The old hot chocolate charged up his throat. He swallowed it back. He felt horrible; he wanted it to stop. He wanted Aki's lights to charge right up to him, and then the trees would just be trees, and the bad things would be pushed back by the light. He wished he'd never come here.

Then the sled wouldn't move. They were stuck. They were caught. He wanted to call out to Johnny, but he didn't know if he could. His throat was dry and sick. He heard a dog bark, somewhere.

Rock barked.

Just once.

And Johnny felt the pull. He felt his sled move, only a tiny bit, a couple of centimetres. But he could feel the strength and effort. Rock's bark had been an order. *Pull.* Johnny was sure of it. Siberian huskies hardly ever barked; Aki had told them that. Johnny got off the sled. His legs went deep into the snow, way over his boots, over his knees. The sled moved forward. He could hear the dogs pant. He held on to the sled, and the stick with the hat. He pushed. His boots got sucked into the snow. He thought they'd come off as he pulled them out. He curled up his toes. He tried to grip the inside of the boots; his socks had slid down. He pushed. Forward, two more steps. He called to Tom.

"OK?"

Tom didn't answer. Johnny looked back. His sled moved. He had to turn back again. His face went right into a line of snow and pine needles. He kept pushing. He pushed his face out of the needles. He called again.

"OK? Tom?"

Tom still didn't answer.

"Tom?"

"Yeah?"

"OK?"

"Where are you?"

"Here."

"Where?"

Rock barked.

"Hear that?" said Johnny.

"Yeah," said Tom. "I can see you."

Johnny's sled moved forward a metre, and stopped. He felt the dogs strain; he felt it in his hands, through his gloves. He pushed. He heard the dogs scrabble and pull.

Tom was off his sled too. It was like pushing straight into a nightmare, going further asleep instead of waking up. He wanted to pull back, even to just let go. Let Hupö and Pomp and the sled go ahead and turn back, to the adults. He heard himself groaning. He sounded like an engine. He pushed, so hard he lifted the sled off the snow. His boots were stuck. He thought he was going to fall forward; he was falling. But his foot came out of the snow; he got it out – the boot was still on it. He stepped forward, and the other foot came out. He kept groaning. It was easier that way. It stopped his teeth from chattering. It helped him feel stronger. He pushed again. He felt the dogs pulling; he heard them panting. He pushed. He felt the sled move. He heard Johnny.

"OK?"

He couldn't see him. But he sounded near.

"Yeah," said Tom.

But it didn't sound loud enough. He took a huge breath and said it again.

"Yeah."

He felt his hat being lifted by the branch right over his head. He felt the sudden cold on his forehead. He could feel the cold on his nose, pushing against it, like a slow fist. He let go of the sled. He grabbed his hat just as it came off his head. He pulled it back over his ears. He could feel loose hard needles in the hat, sticking into his skull. But they didn't hurt too much, and the cold was off his forehead and ears.

The sled slid away before he could grab it. He had to run – he tried to run. He tried to reach the handles of the sled. It moved further. He was being left behind. There was a branch in his way. The sled was gone. He couldn't get past the branch; he couldn't get through. It wouldn't give; it was solid – it wouldn't bend forward. It was like a wall. He couldn't see. He was trapped. He pushed. He groaned. His face was frozen. The branch lashed ice at him; it rubbed the ice right into his skin. He couldn't hear the dogs. He couldn't hear Aki's engine. He hadn't heard it for a good while. Aki and Kalle weren't coming up behind him. There was no one to rescue him. All he could hear was his own breath and the wind. There was wood in his mouth, and dirty ice, and spikes and needles jabbed at his lips and nostrils. He pulled his head back. He put his hand in front of his face. He shouted.

"Johnny!"

He pushed.

He shouted again.

"Johnny!"

"What?"

"I'm stuck."

He cried then. He pushed. He called out to Johnny again.

"My sled's gone."

He heard Johnny.

"I have it."

And that gave him strength; he could feel it. He tried to push a different part of the branch. The tree must have been on his left, because he moved a step to the right and pushed, and the branch wasn't as powerful. It must have been narrower there. He felt it bend; he could feel it give.

He pushed. He even used his face. He pushed straight into the needles and ice, and now he could step forward, and he felt the branch bend and pull back the side of his face as he pushed through it. And then it was gone, behind him. He was out.

The branch sprang back and smacked him hard. He was on his knees. He'd fallen forward. He was gasping. But he was free. He wasn't crying now. He wanted to laugh, but he didn't have breath for it. He tried to stand up. He put his hands on the snow, but they sank. His nose touched the snow. His hands, arms, his feet, legs, were in it. He could feel the cold pull his face.

He got one leg up. He was able to get his foot flat on the ground. He could feel it solid under his boot. He pushed, he straightened the leg. He lifted the other leg. He straightened his arms. He rose over the snow, still on all fours. Then he pushed his hands off the ground. His balance was good. He stood; he stayed standing.

He could see Johnny. He thought he could see him – and the sleds and dogs. He wiped the snow off his face. He pulled his feet out of the snow. It was a path again. The trees were apart. The branches and needles weren't touching him.

Johnny was standing on his brake, leaning over a bit. He was holding one of the straps that held the dogs to Tom's sled. The dogs were quiet. They weren't trying to get away.

"OK?" said Johnny.

"Yeah," said Tom.

The dogs were looking at him. He could see that.

Two more deep steps, and he was back on the sled. And he knew – he suddenly remembered – they had to find their mother. That was why he'd been fighting through the trees. That was why Johnny was waiting for him.

They were alone. There was no one behind them now. They were way off the safe paths, and their mother was even further away. It was only them.

He heard Johnny.

"Ready?"

"Yeah."

"Let's go."

Tom filled his lungs, and let go.

"Wil-derness!"

It sounded brilliant. It sounded big and funny, like the first time they'd shouted it.

He heard Johnny.

"Wil-derness!"

They were moving again, in a straight line. Tom could feel the snow, brushing against and rushing past his face.

He called out to Johnny.

"Maybe she can hear us."

And he heard Johnny shout it again.

"Wil-derness!"

And then it was Tom's turn.

"Wil-derness!"

And Johnny's turn again.

"Wil-derness!"

"Wil-derness!"

They stopped for a second. They put their feet on the brakes, and listened. They heard nothing. They lifted their feet, and the dogs went again. They were moving nicely, and evenly. The boys kept listening, but they heard nothing.

Tom heard Johnny.

"Wil-derness!"

And Tom did it again.

"Wil-derness!"

They kept on doing it, together and apart, in deep voices and cartoon voices, and back to their own voices.

"Wil-derness!"

And the dogs kept running.

And they heard it.

They thought they did.

Johnny put his feet on the brake. Tom waited till his sled was beside Johnny's, then he put his feet on his brake. They could see each other now.

Johnny called out.

"Wil-derness!"

They listened.

Tom called out.

"Wil-derness!"

They listened. And they heard it. Far away, but they definitely heard it.

"Wil-derness!"

It was their mother.

The Kitchen

It was a fight. Two arms, two fists joined, inside her chest. Both pulling, straining. Pushing against her ribs.

She sat still. She concentrated.

"Are you OK?" said her mother.

Gráinne waited a bit. Then she nodded.

It wasn't true, but it was the answer she wanted to give.

"Are you sure?" said her mother.

Gráinne nodded again.

"I'm fine."

"You look a bit pale."

"No," said Gráinne. "I'm fine."

And she began to feel that what she'd said was true. The fists in her chest were fading away. She was still sitting at the table. And her mother was just sitting down, with a fresh mug of tea.

"It's lovely to have decent tea again," she said. "The Americans don't really understand tea."

She looked at Gráinne.

"Will I go on?" she said.

"Not about tea," said Gráinne.

"No," said her mother. "Not tea. I must have sounded like my mother there. Tea, tea, tea."

Gráinne said nothing. The fists were hardly there now. They *were* there; she knew that. But she'd made them move away. Gráinne was controlling it.

"I'll go on?" said her mother.

"Yes," said Gráinne.

"Where did I stop?" said her mother.

That annoyed Gráinne. She knew exactly where her mother had stopped. *I knew what I had to do – what I was doing. And that was what I did. I went.* Word for word, Gráinne knew it. She always would. She knew it, and her mother should have too. Or she was pretending, trying to be casual about it. And that annoyed Gráinne too, because it wasn't honest. But she said nothing. She didn't answer.

"So," said her mother, in a drawn-out way that sounded quite American. "So, I left."

She shrugged.

"And I have to say two things here, and one of them might sound ugly. OK?"

Gráinne nodded.

"I don't regret it," said her mother.

Gráinne could feel the fists again, a sudden burst to the front of her chest. She hoped her face was blank and normal. She could feel sweat, cold, on her forehead. She stayed still.

"I don't regret it," her mother said again. "I feel disgusted, now, saying that. But I have to tell the truth."

Gráinne nodded.

"It was the right thing to do at the time," said her mother. "I'd have done something – I don't know. It couldn't have stayed as it was."

She sighed.

"I don't regret it."

She held her cup. But she didn't drink.

Gráinne waited for the fists inside to get smaller, to retreat. She could hear the clock on the wall. She could hear the fridge. She heard a door upstairs pulled quietly closed. Her father. He was wandering around.

"You said, two things," she said.

She was glad she spoke; she wasn't just waiting. She looked at her mother.

"You said you had to say two things."

"Yes," said her mother.

"Go on."

"Right," said her mother. "Like I said, I don't regret going. But there are lots of things I do regret, because I went."

Her hands on the table opened and closed.

"I regret not being with you," she said. "It sounds so lame, I guess. But it's true. I regretted that even before I left. I remember it, exactly."

She put her hand to her chest.

"It's still in there," she said. "The feeling when I was leaving. Like my ribs were being torn."

She sucked in air; she was trying to keep talking.

"I always felt it."

Gráinne watched her mother's hands. Opening and closing, opening and closing.

"I look at you now, and it's great," said her mother. "I'm here. And you're here. And it kills me."

She cried then. She couldn't talk. She lifted her hands and waved them, as if to say, *I'll be back in a minute*. Then she put her hands to her face and cried. She bawled. Gráinne hadn't seen an adult cry like that before. Her mother was crying like a child. Her face was very white, and blotchy. She looked like she was in pain, like her face was badly made and the different parts didn't fit or match up right.

She rubbed her face with both hands. She stood up. She went across to the counter, beside the cooker. She picked up something. It was the kitchen roll, a big roll of paper. Gráinne watched her blow her nose. She blew twice, then she dropped the paper into the pedal bin. She came back to the table. She sat down.

She looked at Gráinne. She smiled. Her face was normal again, but she looked nervous.

"I feel better," she said. "Will I go on?"

"Yes," said Gráinne.

Her mother put her hands flat on the table.

"So," she said in that American way again. *Soo-ooh*.
"I can hardly cope with it. Seeing you. No, it's great."

She lifted her hands.

"It's wonderful. You can't imagine how wonderful it is."

Gráinne said nothing.

"It's so great," said her mother. "But I missed so much. Do you understand, Gráinne?"

Gráinne liked her mother – she knew that now. But she didn't like this – the way she'd said her name, the way she'd asked Gráinne if she understood.

"Yes, I understand," said Gráinne. "How do you think I felt?"

Her mother stared at her.

"I'm sorry," she said. "I'm sorry."

"Why didn't you visit?" said Gráinne.

"I should have."

"Why didn't you?"

"Guilt," said her mother.

"Guilt?"

"Yes."

"Are you serious?" said Gráinne.

Her mother was surprised; Gráinne could see.

"Yes," she said. "I am."

The fists were beating at Gráinne's chest, trying to break out. They were good now; they were like a warning. *Calm down, calm down*.

"Go on," she said.

"Well," said her mother. "I did the right thing, leaving. But it was a terrible thing to do. I know that. And that was how I felt. It was bad. *I* was bad. Abandoning my child."

"Me," said Gráinne.

"You."

"Why did you go so far away?"

"It had to be far," said her mother. "That was what I thought. I felt that you'd be better off without me. You and your dad. Especially you."

"You didn't even visit," said Gráinne.

"I couldn't."

"Yes, you could," said Gráinne.

"You're right," said her mother. "I was dying to see you. To be with you. But I couldn't do it. I felt so guilty. I thought it would be better if it was like I was dead."

"But you weren't dead."

"No."

"So, it was just stupid," said Gráinne.

She didn't shout; she just said it.

Her mother opened her mouth. But she didn't speak.

"I knew you weren't dead," said Gráinne. "And there's no such thing as 'like dead'. I knew you were alive. And you never came to see me. You never asked for me."

"I'm sorry," said her mother.

"OK."

"I'm sorry."

"I always thought it was because of me."

"What?" said her mother.

"Why you left," said Gráinne. "I thought it was because of me."

"No," said her mother. "Believe me, Gráinne. It was never like that."

"And you never came home," said Gráinne.

"It's a mess," said her mother.

She sighed.

"Your grandmother sent me photographs, and she told me how you were doing in school."

A snort came from Gráinne's nose. She nearly laughed.

"You should see my apartment, Gráinne. It's full of pictures of you."

"So what?" said Gráinne. "My room's full of pictures of Marilyn Manson, but that doesn't mean I know him. Or even care about him that much."

She wished the light was off. It would have been easier. Her head was hurting, just behind her eyes. She was tired too, and thirsty. She wished it would finish. She wanted it to stop.

But it was too soon; she knew that. They had to keep going.

"Can you forgive me?" said her mother.

"Why are you here?" said Gráinne.

"To see you," said her mother.

"Just see?"

"No," said her mother. "I want to know you. Be with you."

"Why now?"

"I've always wanted—"

"Why *now*?"

"A friend of mine died."

"What kind of friend?"

"My best friend, Gráinne."

She smiled. She shrugged.

"We went to school together."

"Did I ever meet her?" said Gráinne.

"I'm not sure," said her mother. "Yes. Yes. You did. She came to see me. She stayed here for a little while after you were born."

"Did she live in New York?"

"Yes."

"Did you live with her?"

"No."

"When you went over?"

"For a few weeks, yes."

"What was her name?" said Gráinne.

"Bernie," said her mother.

"I'm sorry she died," said Gráinne.

"Thank you."

Gráinne didn't have a friend like that. She didn't really have friends at all.

"Anyway," said her mother. "She told me she had cancer, and five weeks later I was at her funeral. Standing beside her husband and her son. And I knew I'd made a terrible mistake and that I had to come here and see you and try – I don't know. Make amends? Start again? Say hello?"

She smiled; she cried. She wiped her eyes. She looked at Gráinne.

Gráinne nodded.

CHAPTER ELEVEN

"Wil-derness!"

They shouted into the dark, but nothing came back. They listened; they leaned forward on the sleds. They'd only heard her once.

"Where did it come from?" said Tom.

He meant their mother's voice.

"Over there," said Johnny. "I think."

Tom looked, and could just make out where Johnny's arm was pointing.

"Wil-derness!"

Nothing.

"Wil-derness!"

"What will we do?" said Johnny.

"Just go," said Tom.

"Yeah," said Johnny.

"The dogs will find her," said Tom.

"Yeah," said Johnny. "Ready?"

"Ready when you are, my friend," said Tom.

He was scared. But he felt good. They'd heard their mother's voice. They weren't lost. They'd nearly found her. He heard Johnny scraping ice off the metal plates, where he put his feet. Tom did the same. He took one foot off the brake and knocked the ice off the plate with his boot. They got ready for the last push.

He heard, and saw, Johnny's sled advance. He took his feet off the brake, and he was moving. They were on good snow now, and the dogs were soon moving fast. There was space between the trees.

"Wil-derness!"

Nothing.

"Wilder-nessss!"

They followed the dogs. The snow was thick again, crashing into their faces. Johnny's hands were freezing cold, even inside his gloves. He had to tell his fingers to move – he even said it out loud. They were so stiff, sore. He couldn't feel the stick that held Kalle's hat. That part of his hand was numb, like it was welded to the sled.

They kept going.

"Wil-derness!"

Tom watched the dogs' backs. He tried to get ready for jumps or bends. He tried to see ahead. But they were in the trees again, and it was even darker. He used his elbows and arms like shields against the grabbing branches.

They kept going.

"Wilder-ness!"

They heard it, together. They heard her voice. It was near, and miles away. It was left, right, straight ahead, behind them – they didn't know from where.

Johnny stopped.

Tom stopped.

Johnny shouted.

"Wil-derness!"

They heard her again.

"Shout something else!"

It was definitely their mother.

"Something else!" Johnny shouted back.

Tom laughed. His throat was dry, so it sounded like a bark.

They heard her again.

"I'm over here!"

"Where?!"

"Here!"

Tom saw Johnny's outstretched arm.

"Over there," said Johnny.

Tom agreed. Her voice had come from that direction. Left, and forward, behind what looked like a black mountain of trees.

"How do we make the dogs go that way?" said Tom.

"We don't," said Johnny. "It's the way Rock's been bringing us all along."

He was right. It was another surprise, although Tom had always known it. Rock had led them this far, and

he'd bring them the rest of the way. That was it –
Johnny and Tom could make the sleds stop and go,
but it was Rock who decided where they went. And
Rock had decided to help them find their mother.

A branch slapped Johnny's face; he didn't care.

"Where are you?" he shouted.

She didn't answer; they didn't hear her. They were
in the black trees now, and another branch lashed
across the side of Johnny's face. Snow had gone down
the back of his suit; he could feel it rolling and
melting on his back.

"Where are you?!"

No answer.

The dogs kept running. Tom could see each tree.
They were different trees, and the bottom branches
were way above their heads. Maybe she couldn't hear
them; their voices were trapped beneath the
branches. Tom shouted again.

"Hell-ohh!"

Nothing.

It was warmer and quiet here, beneath the tall
trees. But Johnny wanted to get out. It was too like
being in a cave. Like a new, high wall between him
and his mother. She was very near – he knew it – but
he couldn't hear or see her. The snow was thin here;
Johnny could feel that in his feet. The sled vibrated
over solid ground as the dogs dragged him further
under the trees.

"Hell-ohh!"

No answer.

They were out of the trees. The snow was on them again. He heard Tom.

"Wil-derness!"

The word in the air was like hope coming back.

"Wilder-ness!"

They heard her. Johnny heard her. He definitely heard her voice. There was an echo of it, a memory, and it seemed to be right in front of him. They were on a slope, going down. He had to lean towards the hill, his whole weight, to stop the sled from toppling over. He couldn't shout; he had to concentrate.

Tom was suddenly on the hill, suddenly going down. He thought he was falling off. But he saw what was happening. He saw the slope and Johnny's sled in front of him and, before he decided, he was leaning into the hill, his right leg bent, and he stayed that way until they were off the slope, and they were going along a valley, slopes now on both sides. They could stand straight on the sleds. They could shout again.

"Wilder-ness!"

"Wilder-ness!"

"Lads!"

They saw her dogs before they saw their mother. There were four of them, and it looked as if they were climbing all over a fallen log. Then they saw her lying in the snow, away from the log.

"I can see you!" Johnny shouted.

They'd found her.

They came closer to the log. Her sled was broken and on its side, and the straps were tangled in the branches that were jutting from the log. Her dogs were trying to free themselves. And, as they came closer, one dog became more frantic. They watched and heard him trying to bite through the leather straps that had him trapped. It was Hastro.

Their mother was lying on the slope. She was lying beside a boulder that was almost buried in the snow.

"Hiya, lads," she said.

Her voice sounded weak and wavy, as if she'd been shivering when she spoke.

It scared Tom. She hadn't got up to hug them. She'd just turned her head, to look.

It scared Johnny. She hadn't moved at all. He stopped his sled. He didn't want to bring it any closer. He put his feet on the brake, made sure the steel teeth were deep in the snow. He stepped off the sled. Tom did the same. He jumped on the brake, to bury the teeth down deep. And he stepped back, off the sled. He put his feet into the snow.

Hastro was snarling and whining, and dragging the other dogs with him. But he was getting nowhere. He was tangling the straps even more.

The boys went the last deep steps to where their

mother lay. They lifted their feet out of the snow; they made sure they didn't fall.

"Hiya, lads," she said again.

"Are you OK?" said Johnny.

"I'm grand," she said. "But I think I'm after breaking something."

"What?" said Johnny.

"My leg," she said. "I think. Hiya, Tom."

"Hi," said Tom.

He saw her smile. Her arm came up, although she didn't move much. He saw her hand. She wanted to hold his hand. She looked at Johnny. She wanted his hand too. They did it at the same time. They let themselves drop to their knees, and they landed right beside her.

She laughed – she tried to laugh.

"You're great lads," she said. "Where are the others?"

Then they heard it.

And they saw it.

Rock had pulled his sled, even with the brake teeth dragging piles of snow. He'd pulled it right up to Hastro. He stood now, right over Hastro, right on top of him. His paw was on Hastro's head, and his mouth was full of Hastro's neck. There was a yelp – it was the first thing they'd heard, before they saw anything. It was Hastro that had yelped. And there was a growl. That was Rock.

The boys didn't move. Rock stopped growling. He didn't move. Hastro didn't move. None of the other dogs moved. It was total silence – white silence. Rock stood over Hastro, with his teeth holding his neck.

Johnny whispered.

"He's teaching him a lesson."

"Yeah," said Tom.

He'd thought at first it was going to be horrible, that he'd have to watch one dog killing the other one. But then he knew it wasn't going to be like that. Without shifting his legs or paws, Rock lifted his head from Hastro's neck. They watched as Hastro stood, making sure he didn't touch Rock. He had to crawl out from under him. He was still trapped in the straps, tied up to the fallen log. He had hardly any room as he got back up on all four legs. But he didn't touch Rock. Rock was the lead dog, and he was making sure that Hastro knew it.

"Cool," said Tom, very quietly.

"That was amazing," said Johnny.

They looked down at their mother, and they knew it wasn't over. It was only beginning. She was shivering now, her whole body. They could hear her teeth chattering. She was trying to smile, but they could tell that she was frightened.

It was weird. It was terrible. Tom had expected her to hug him when they'd found her. He'd been cold and tired and very frightened. He was a kid; she was his mother. But she was lying on the snow, and she was broken and sick.

And something happened.

He knew what to do. He just did. He knew what had to be done.

"Fire," he said.

"Yeah," said Johnny.

It had happened to Johnny too. He thought it was the dogs, being alone with the dogs. Being with the dogs had changed him. He was still a kid, but he'd become something else as well. He'd been alone. He'd learned from the dogs. He knew how to survive. He just knew it.

"Wood," he said.

Tom was already getting up. He broke small twigs off the fallen log. But they were damp. They'd take ages to light. He waded through the snow, to where some trees were close together. The twigs and needles around the trunks were dry and almost crispy. He filled his arms.

They couldn't move their mother. It was dangerous to move someone with a broken leg; it would only make it worse. Johnny was pushing snow away, trying to clear a gap for the fire beside his mother. He was sweating and cold. He could feel the ground through his gloves, but he couldn't see it yet. He sat, and pushed with his boots. He did a full circle. It was good they weren't too near a tree. Not because it might catch fire. Aki had told them, the snow sometimes slid off the branches, right on to the fire. He cleared the snow, right up to his mother's side, where she lay.

Tom dropped his first load in the space that Johnny had cleared.

"I'll get bigger sticks and branches too," he said. "For when the fire's going."

"Yeah," said Johnny. "Good."

His mother had gone very quiet. She was too quiet. Johnny knew – they'd have to keep her awake. They'd have to make her talk and answer.

"Are you OK?" he said.

He gently pushed her shoulder.

"Hi," she said.

He heard her teeth.

"Are you OK?" he said.

"I'm grand."

She closed her eyes. He pushed her shoulder again.

"Don't go asleep," he said.

Tom came back and dropped more wood and needles.

She opened her eyes.

"You're not to go to sleep," said Johnny.

"I'm cold," she said.

"We're making a fire," said Johnny.

"Great," she said. "That's great."

He had to keep her talking.

"What happened?" he said.

"What?"

"What happened? How did it happen?"

"Oh," she said. "The usual."

She closed her eyes. He pushed her shoulder.

"The bloody dog," she said. "What's his name –"

"Hastro."

"Yeah, Castro."

"Hastro," said Johnny.

"Him," said his mother. "We were way behind everyone. Then, whoosh."

"What?"

"He took off. Swerved off the path. And the other bow-wows went with him."

"Were you scared?"

Tom was back, with bigger pieces of wood.

"Good man, Tom," she said.

"Were you scared?" Johnny asked again.

He helped Tom with the wood. They made a small hill of the twigs and needles.

"They won't last," said Tom.

"Yeah," said Johnny. "But they'll start it. Were you scared?" he asked his mother.

She moved her head slightly – that was good – so she could look at them while she spoke.

"No," she said. "Not really. But, like, I've been scared since we got here."

Tom had unzipped the front of his suit. He took his knife out, from the pocket in his jeans.

"Where did that come from?" said his mother.

"I bought it," said Tom. "With my own money."

"You should have told me."

"You'd have said no," said Johnny. "And we'd be in trouble because we didn't have a knife."

"OK," said their mother. "You win."

Tom was slicing the wood, the same way Aki had done it. He cut around the end of the branch, so it looked like a mad haircut, or a pineapple.

Their mother was closing her eyes again. They could see the shivers running through her, even in the dark. They could hear them.

Johnny leaned over and tapped her shoulder.

"What happened then?"

"What?"

"What happened? When Hastro swerved away."

"Yeah," she said. "I didn't know. Not at first. I thought he was taking a shortcut."

The boys laughed; they couldn't help it. She enjoyed it; they could see it in her face.

"And it wasn't that long, you know," she said. "Between then, and here. I don't think we came that far."

"It took us ages," said Tom.

"Yeah," said Johnny.

"Well, it didn't feel long when it happened," she said. "But, God, lads. It was mad."

Tom had given punk haircuts to three of the

branches. The fresh-cut parts would take the fire more easily, and the fire would climb the rest of the branch.

They'd made a pile of twigs and needles, and a tepee of punk branches right over it.

Then he thought of something.

"We've no way to light it," he said.

It was like being smacked on the head. Tom suddenly felt tired again, and annoyed.

"Oh, yes, we do," said Johnny.

"How?" said Tom. "There's no sun and, anyway, we don't have a magnifying glass."

"Shut up a sec."

"Or flints."

"Shut up."

Tom was really annoyed, too angry to be frightened. He wanted to kick and shout. But something stopped him. Something about the way Johnny had spoken. And something else as well, that settled in his head – they'd done all this together, him and Johnny. They'd found their mother. Now Johnny had an idea. It was like Johnny's voice had grabbed Tom's anger and gently pulled it back. He wanted to hear, to find out what they had to do.

He looked at Johnny.

"What?" he said.

Johnny turned to his mother. He nudged her shoulder. Her eyes stayed shut. He shook her.

She looked at him.

"I should stay awake," she chattered. "Right?"

"Right," said Johnny. "We need to light the fire."

She held her mouth still – she tried to – for a second, then she spoke.

"That's grand."

"OK," said Johnny. "But, you know the way you pretend you don't smoke?"

Tom nearly laughed. He'd forgotten, completely.

"I don't," she said.

She stopped.

"OK," she said.

"Where do you hide your lighter?"

"Pocket."

"Which one?" said Johnny.

She lifted her right hand – she was able to – very slowly, and she tapped the pocket at the side of the trousers part of the suit.

"You do it," she said. "I can't. I can't feel my fingers."

Tom heard the scratching sound. Johnny unzipped the pocket.

"I promise not to tickle you," he told her, and he put his hand into the pocket.

"I love you, boys," she said.

She smiled – she tried to.

They had to work fast. She was falling asleep again.

"Got it," said Johnny.

The lighter fell out of his hands, into the snow. He grabbed at it, and had it in his glove again.

"I'll have to take the gloves off first," he said. "Hold it a sec."

Tom took the lighter, and watched Johnny take his gloves off.

"No," said Johnny, like he was thinking out loud.

He looked at Tom.

"You do it," he said. "You're better at it than me."

It was true. Tom could always light matches better than Johnny. They never broke. And he could always make lighters go, first time.

He pulled off his gloves and dropped them. His fingers were freezing. He put the lighter on a glove and rubbed his hands together, really hard. He picked up the lighter. It was a white plastic one, with an ad for a pub or something on the side. He put his thumb on the small metal wheel, the thing that would spark the flint. He lay on his stomach and chest – he did it all really quickly. He put the top of the lighter just under a couple of twigs. He pulled his thumb down, hard, against the wheel.

"Yes!"

The flame – it came first time. He watched it chew and crawl along the twig. It jumped to another twig, and another. He watched it grow. He got his face away from the fire. They wouldn't have to blow, to keep it lit. The snow was falling on it, but the fire reached a branch's haircut and began to slowly eat it – and another branch. The snow wasn't heavy and soon they could hear the little hiss as each flake fell into the fire.

"Good job," said Johnny.

"Thanks," said Tom.

He put the lighter into one of his pockets. He zipped it.

They ran to the trees and came back with their arms full of needles and twigs and small sticks. They moved the branches, so the flames would catch the higher branch, and climb. They found more branches and made a pile of them near the fire, but not too near. They didn't want to start another fire.

Johnny was on his knees now, beside his mother, away from the fire, so he wouldn't get in the way of the heat, or burn his boots and feet. Tom got down beside him. Their mother's eyes were closed again.

Johnny shook her.

"Wake up."

He shook again.

"Wake up."

He put his cold glove on her cheek. Her eyes still didn't open. He got some snow and put it on her neck. She didn't wake. She might have been too cold, as cold as snow, already. He tried again, more snow on her neck. He rubbed it on. He took off his glove and put his hand on her neck. He rubbed. And Tom rubbed her forehead. He got some snow and rubbed it across her skin.

They felt her move.

"God," she said.

Her eyes were open. She felt the heat. She looked.

"Look at that," she said.

"Can you move over on your side?" said Johnny.

"I'll try," she said.

They heard her gasp.

"Give me a hand, lads," she said. "But don't roll me into the fire."

"Hang on," said Johnny.

The ground in front of the fire was wet and getting softer. It would soon be like a swamp. The boys went over the snow, and came back with armfuls of pine needles. They put them, spread them, on the ground. They checked to make sure she was still awake. They went back for more, and more. They made a bed for their mother, and themselves.

They put their hands under her shoulder and side, and pushed her up and a little forward, and helped her lie on her side, and on the needles. She gasped, and groaned. They knew she was in pain, every time she moved. But she was facing the fire, and she'd hardly moved her legs.

"Lovely," she said. "Cuddle up to me, boys."

"Wait," said Johnny.

They untangled her dogs. They released their own dogs from their sleds. The dogs were quiet. They rubbed against the boys' hands. It was hard to tell which of them was Hastro, except for his different-coloured eyes. He kept well away from Rock.

The boys tied the dogs' straps to the fallen tree.

"We've no food for them," said Tom.

"Our ones ate their dinner before we left the hut."

"But Mam's," said Tom.

"They'll just have to wait till tomorrow," said Johnny. "And it serves them right."

Tom laughed.

"No dessert for them fellas," he said. "Are you hungry?" he then said, seriously.

"No," said Johnny.

"Me neither," said Tom.

But they both were.

They went back to their mother. She was still awake. She held up the arm that wasn't under her body.

"Come on," she said. "Take turns."

Tom got there first. He didn't push, and Johnny didn't try to stop him. Tom lay down in front of his mother, right against her, with his back to her tummy. He did it gently, so he wouldn't do anything to her broken leg. Her arm went around him, and Tom felt the happiest feeling he'd had in all his life. His pillow was soggy muck and slush; it was horrible on his face. But that didn't matter. They'd saved their mother, and now her arm was around him. She was his mother again, and he was a different boy. That was how he felt. He'd done something tonight that had changed him. The achievement rested in his tummy, like great food, and in his head, like a brilliant joke he'd be able to tell again and again. And he loved it.

Johnny sat beside them, close to his mother's face. The needles were still dry; he was pleased with that. He wanted to lie down. He want to cuddle up to his mother too. But he was the older brother, and he liked that. He liked that he was the only one not lying down.

"What happened then?" he said.

His mother lifted her head, so she could rest it on his leg. She moved her head again, a bit, and looked up at him.

"What?" she said.

"What happened after Hastro broke away?"

"Well, I went with him," she said. "Like, I didn't want to be rude."

The boys laughed, and she felt Tom's laughter in her arm, right through her, and in Johnny's leg.

"I don't know what happened exactly," she said. "The sled hit something, and I landed on that rock there. And I heard it."

She groaned.

"The ol' leg," she said. "Not nice. I think the sound was worse than the pain, though. But the pain was bad. The shock, though; God."

She was able to talk without stopping and gasping, or trying to make her lips and tongue obey her.

They heard her sigh.

"And here we are, lads," she said. "On our picnic. And what about you fellas?"

"What?"

"What happened you?" she said. "How did you find me?"

They told her the lot. They took turns; they didn't bash into each other's words. They told her about going into the hut, and how she wasn't there. They told her about Kalle and Aki going first, and coming back without her. They told her about sneaking out of the hut, and about the hut as well, because she hadn't seen it. They told her about taking Kalle's hat, and hitching the dogs to the sleds, and making them go by dangling the hat in front of Rock's nose, and about their journey through the dark, about the lights of Aki's snowmobile behind them, but how they kept going because they wanted to find her more than anyone, and about their fight through the branches and the dark, and how they'd shouted, and how they'd heard her, and how they'd kept going and shouting until they found her.

"God, lads," she said. "You're amazing. Both of you."

By now, Johnny was lying beside them. They were like a sandwich, and Tom was the cheese or meat, between his mother and Johnny. It was hours and hours to daylight – they didn't know what time it was. They didn't know how long they'd have to wait, or how long the wood would last.

Johnny stood up, to put more of the wood on the fire. He gently dropped two large branches on to it. It was still a good fire.

"That was a stroke of genius, though," said his mother.

"What was?" said Johnny.

"Using Kalle's hat," she said. "For the scent."

"Yeah," Tom agreed. "It wouldn't have worked without the hat."

He'd nearly been asleep, but he was awake again.

"That was Johnny," he said. "He thought of it."

"Brilliant," she said. "And Rock followed the hat all the way."

"Yeah," said Tom.

"No," said Johnny.

"What?"

Johnny went over to the sled – they watched him – and he picked up the stick.

"No hat," he said.

Tom could see him clearly in the firelight. Johnny was holding up the stick. Kalle's hat wasn't there, at the end of it. And he knew; Johnny wasn't messing. It wasn't on the ground, and Johnny hadn't hidden it.

"When did it fall off?" Tom asked.

"Don't know," said Johnny.

"Hang on," said their mother. "Does that mean he came on his own? Without the scent?"

"Yeah," said Johnny.

He went across and patted Rock. All the dogs were lying down. They'd made beds in the snow.

"God," said their mother. "That's a bit spooky."

"It's brilliant," said Tom.

"I know," she said. "I know. But, like, it doesn't make sense."

"Only if you're not a dog," said Tom.

She kissed the back of his head.

"I love you, mister," she said. "And you too, Johnny."

"And Rock," said Tom.

"And Rock," said their mother.

"Can we get a dog when we go home?" said Tom.

"No," said their mother.

"Ah –"

"OK, OK, OK," she said. "Yes."

"A husky?"

"Can you get them at home?"

"Yeah," said Tom.

"Right so," said their mother. "For Christmas."

"Cool."

But they weren't home yet. They knew it. Johnny put more wood on the fire. He lay back down on the ground. He swapped places with Tom. Tom was nearer the fire, and Johnny was nearer his mother. It was his turn.

"You're special," she said, very quietly, just for him.

They watched the fire. They fell asleep, one at a time. They woke with a shock – the cold, the fire.

They slept again. They woke. They listened. The boys got up and fed more of the wood to the fire. There wasn't much left. They lay down. They dreamed. They woke.

They slept.

Johnny woke.

Something had rubbed against him. In his sleep, while he was still in his dream – something rubbed. Fur, breath.

He woke.

He didn't move.

He saw them.

The dogs.

The dogs were lying all around them. Around Johnny, Tom, their mother. Behind them, and in front. They'd come as far as their straps would let them.

Johnny looked. His mother's eyes were open.

"Amazing," she whispered.

"They stink," said Johnny.

"Yep."

They lay awake. Tom snored, just once. Like a furry bullet. Johnny and his mother grinned – they felt each other grinning. They closed their eyes.

Johnny could feel the snow, on his face. It was heavier again. He kept his eyes shut. He didn't look at the fire.

The Door

Her mother had opened the front door, but she closed it again.

"Well," she said.

She kept her hand on the latch.

"This has been great," she said.

They were going to see each other again. They were meeting the day after next, in town. They were going to see a lot of each other. Gráinne would go to New York, sometimes. Her mother would come home twice a year.

A few minutes earlier, when they were sitting in the kitchen, her mother had suggested that Gráinne come and live with her in New York. Gráinne had said no.

Her mother had cried a little, but she'd nodded.

"It was just an idea," she'd said.

"Yeah," said Gráinne. "It's cool."

It was dark now. Gráinne was standing beside the switch. She turned on the light. They were suddenly bright and blinking.

Her mother laughed, then stopped. She let go of the latch. She lifted her arms and put them around Gráinne.

Gráinne didn't hug her back. She couldn't do it; she didn't really want to. But she let herself be hugged. She heard her mother sniff. She could smell her mother's soap. She felt the arms come away, and she saw her mother wipe her eyes, and smile.

"I'm crying too much," she said.

She pushed her hair back from her forehead. There were bits of grey in her hair. Gráinne thought it was cool. It looked kind of deliberate, the same colour as her jacket.

"Well," said her mother, again.

She put her hand on the latch. Gráinne heard the click. The door was open. She heard the outside noises getting louder.

"I'll phone you," said her mother. "Tomorrow night. Right?"

Gráinne nodded.

Her mother stepped back a bit, so she could open the door properly. She looked at Gráinne. And then she looked away, past Gráinne, and up a bit – up the stairs.

"Hello, Frank," she said.

She smiled.

Gráinne turned, and saw her father on the stairs, two steps down from the landing.

"Hello," he said.

"You're looking well," said her mother. "I forgot to tell you."

"Thanks," said Frank. "Rosemary. You too."

The phone rang in the kitchen.

He came down the rest of the stairs. He got around the bannister without touching Gráinne or knocking the pile of jackets and hoodies that always hung there. He smiled – he tried to.

"Excuse me," he said.

He went down to the kitchen.

It was weird, Gráinne thought. These people were strangers and, still, they were her parents. She'd have to get used to it. Actually, she thought she liked it. Two parents, two cities, two different countries.

The phone stopped ringing. He'd picked it up.

"I'm definitely going this time," said her mother.

She smiled. Gráinne smiled.

She wanted to go to her father. She wanted to tell him she wasn't leaving, but she didn't know if she could. They said so little to each other. Maybe he wanted her gone.

She knew that wasn't true.

"'Bye," she said.

"'Bye," said her mother.

She leaned across and kissed Gráinne's cheek.

"My honey-boo," she said.

Gráinne remembered the name. It rushed to the

back of her eyes. Her mother used to call her that. *How's my honey-boo; here's my honey-boo.*

Her mother stepped out, to the porch.

"See you very soon," she said.

She held the car keys. She had Gráinne's granny's car.

"Yeah," said Gráinne. "See you."

She started to close the door. She wanted to see her dad. She needed to go down there, to the kitchen.

The car was parked out on the road. Gráinne could see it, behind the hedge.

She closed the door.

She didn't want to.

She closed it. She let go of the latch. She stayed still.

She heard the car, the bleep of the lock. She heard the car door.

She walked away from the door. She went down to the kitchen.

She saw her dad putting the phone down.

He turned. He looked frightened, or something.

"They're missing," he said.

He looked as if he was listening to himself, like he was testing what he'd said.

"They're missing," he said, again. "Sandra and the boys. They've gone missing."

CHAPTER TWELVE

They woke in painful cold. They woke together. So quickly, so cold – they couldn't know they'd been asleep. They were fully awake, and cold. They moved – both boys moved; they heard each other. They were stiff, and numb, and hungry, and shaking.

They were covered in snow. They were under a layer of snow. They could feel it, stiff, even on their eyes. They felt it when they blinked. Johnny moved, his arms and knees. It fell away – his knees and elbows broke through the snow, and he got on to his hands and knees, and stood.

It was still dark but something about it, the grey shape of each tree, the dogs standing all around them, told the boys that it was morning.

Their mother was still asleep. She was covered in snow. She was asleep –

They got down quickly, back down on the snow.

They tried to wake her. But she was stiff, and didn't move or wake when they nudged and pushed her.

They didn't speak – they were afraid to. They didn't want to speak before she did.

Tom brushed all the snow off her, from her cap to her boots. Johnny rubbed her face. He took off his gloves and rubbed both her cheeks. Tom watched him. He watched her; he watched her eyes. He put his hands on her shoulders. He watched her eyes. He rubbed her shoulders. He heard the dogs. He rubbed. And Johnny rubbed. They didn't know what else to do. There was the fire and the wood, but they had to hear her first; they had to see her open her eyes. Tom heard the dogs. Whimpering, prowling, pulling against their straps. He looked at Johnny. He looked at his mother.

They opened.

Her eyes were open.

She was there. Her eyes were open. She was looking at nothing.

The dogs were howling and whimpering. There was another noise.

Her eyes were open but she didn't move. Then she started to shake. It was terrible – electric. Like a shock going through her that wouldn't stop.

The noise – Tom knew it. He didn't look. He couldn't take his eyes off his mother. The shock ran through her, and through her. She didn't blink. She stared at nothing. Her face was dirty white. Johnny kept rubbing.

She moaned.

She moaned. They heard her. Tom heard it now – the engine. Aki's engine. The snowmobile.

His mother moaned. Her mouth must have moved, her lips. They heard her teeth.

They heard her.

"God."

They heard her again.

"Boys."

It didn't sound like her. It wasn't just her shivering. It sounded like she couldn't see them, like she was looking into total blackness and she couldn't see.

Tom did it – he had to. He stood up. He knew he had to do it; he had to start the fire. He had to find the wood. She needed heat. She needed fire. He could hear the engine, but he didn't know how far away, or where. Tom and Johnny were still on their own. The dogs were howling but Aki wouldn't hear them.

There was new snow, loose and high. Tom had to climb through it. He couldn't hear Aki's engine. His own breathing and gasping were all he could hear. He could see his breath; he walked into it. He went past the trees they'd reached the night before. He had to go further. He found more wood, branches that weren't soggy. He gathered up a pile of needles and twigs. He went back to the fire. He didn't rush; he tried not to. He'd fall. He'd have to start again. He wouldn't be able to hold the lighter properly, or spark the fire. His hands were numb; they were sore. He could hear the engine.

Johnny heard it too. He was at the fire, on his stomach. There was a small flame, a tiny, really tiny, orange light; it was going out, getting even smaller. He heard the engine. He was going to run, and shout, to where he thought the sound was coming from.

But he didn't. He stayed where he was.

He knew. He could get up and run and pretend he was going to the rescue. But, really, he'd be running away. Running would be easier than what he had to do. He had to stay. He couldn't wait or run for adults.

The pile of branches, the tepee they'd made over the fire the night before, was partly burnt, but it had stayed standing and acted like a roof when the snow was falling. The fire had survived. The tiny flame – the spark.

He had to blow. But he was afraid to. Too strong, he'd blow it out. Too weak, he'd watch it die. It wouldn't be easy to get a second fire going. His face was in the ashes.

He blew. Nothing – it did nothing. He blew. The orange flickered, but it didn't seem to change. He found some needles beside his chin. They felt hard and dry. He brought them slowly to the flame, just beside it. And he blew. He watched the flame shift.

He watched a needle light, and curl. His free hand felt for more.

He saw Tom's feet. He heard, then saw Tom stretch down beside him.

"Good job," said Tom.

Johnny held some needles to the flame. It grabbed them. He held more. And more – a bigger bundle. It was a fire now, nearly a proper fire. He stood up, carefully. He didn't want to move too fast, create a breeze and put the fire out.

Tom was dropping needles on the fire. He got up on his knees and started adjusting the wood. He wouldn't have to pass the test; he wouldn't have to do it. That was what Tom kept thinking. He wouldn't have to start the fire. It had scared him, all the way back from the trees. But he could feel the heat now. He could hear Aki's engine. He thought it was nearer – he wasn't sure. The fire would be roaring when the snowmobile slid over the hill, and down the slope. He'd adjust the logs and branches, before he went back for more. He lifted one – and the tepee collapsed.

He couldn't believe it. The fire was gone – dead, under the branches. He pulled them away. He didn't care – he didn't care if he burned himself. He pulled them away. He saw the flame. He got down on his stomach. Ashes blew into his face. He could taste it – them. He didn't care; he didn't cough. He kept his eye on the orange flame. He found some needles that hadn't been burnt. He held them in his fist.

Johnny rubbed his mother's face.

Her eyes opened.

They saw nothing. They closed.

Tom watched the flame. And then it wasn't there. It was a while before he realized. The flame wasn't in front of him. There was no little orange flicker.

Johnny rubbed his mother's face.

Tom took off his gloves. He got the lighter from his pocket. He could hardly feel it; his hands were freezing. He put it down – he kind of dropped it. He rubbed his hands; he blew into them. He stretched his fingers. He rubbed and blew again. He picked up the lighter. He could feel it now. He could feel its shape and plastic. He put it beside the little pile of needles. The side of his thumb was on the wheel. He could feel the metal, pressing, biting into his thumb. He closed his eyes. He opened them. He pulled his thumb down, hard, against the wheel.

Nothing.

He did it again.

He heard Johnny.

"What happened to the fire?"

Tom did it again. Nothing – no flame – came from the top of the lighter.

"What happened to the fire?"

Again – he did it again. He shoved his thumb right

against the wheel. He felt the burn – he smelled his skin – before he saw the yellow flame pour sideways from the lighter. The flame licked over his thumb. He didn't care. He held the lighter under the needles. Johnny was beside him, and he helped. He built up the needles. The flame grabbed at needles and twigs and bigger twigs. It began to jump and climb.

Tom took his thumb from his mouth. He put it into the snow. It didn't take the pain away; it wasn't fading. It was horrible.

He stood up. He had to get more wood.

Johnny tried to lift her, so she'd face the fire. His hands kept slipping. He got her up a little bit, enough to get his knees against her, so she was tilted towards the heat.

He watched Tom put branches, criss-crossed, over and around the fire. He felt the heat on his face. He felt his mother's face. He looked at his fingers. He pressed. He lifted his hand. He pressed again. His hands were sore; he couldn't feel anything else. He looked at the skin on her cheek. There were no marks where his fingers had pressed.

The fire was big now.

Tom started to cry.

Her eyes were open before Johnny noticed.

She was looking at the fire. He saw her eyes move. She was looking at Tom.

"What's wrong, Tom?" she said.

"Nothing," said Tom.

He sat beside her. He rubbed his eyes with the sleeve of his suit. He felt the dirt and ashes drag across his face.

"Sure?" she said.

"Yeah," he said. "I'm fine."

They watched the fire.

And that was how Kalle found them. He saw the fire and, as he brought his sled down the slope, he saw the family beside the fire. The boys looked at him and waved.

He liked those boys. He waved back.

Aki was behind Kalle, on the snowmobile, and there were other people too, on sleds. It all began, the action. Their camp was full of people who knew exactly what to do.

But, really, it was over. The boys were on Kalle's sled, covered in blankets. They watched as their mother was lifted on to a special ambulance sled.

Aki was standing beside them.

"They bring her to the lake," he said. "Very slowly, I guess. Carefully. The helicopter will lift her. To the hospital. We'll bring you there."

They heard her.

"Lads?"

"Yeah?" Tom shouted.

"See you in a little while," she said.

They saw her hand wave. They saw the ambulance woman put it back under her blanket.

"See you," said Johnny.

"Bye," said Tom.

He wanted to go with her. But he wanted to stay. He wanted to be here. He wanted to go back with Kalle, through the wilderness.

The rescue woman and man climbed the hill, on each side of their mother's sled. They held it straight as the dogs – there were ten of them – pulled it slowly up the slope.

"Guys."

It was Aki.

He sat on the snowmobile. The engine was off. He waited until both boys were looking at him. Then he spoke.

"She would have died," he said. "You saved her life."

He bowed his head. He smiled.

"I salute you."

He turned on the engine. He turned the snowmobile, and they watched him climb the hill, after the ambulance sled. He went over the top. They could see the lights, then he was gone.

They felt the weight behind them. Kalle had stepped on to the runners.

Johnny shifted a bit, so he could look back, and up, at Kalle.

"How did you find us?" he asked.

Kalle said nothing at first. Johnny watched him put his hand into his pocket. Tom was watching too.

Kalle took his hand out.

They saw it. His hat.

Kalle pointed in the direction Aki had just taken.

"I – find – it," he said. "I – know."

"Cool," said Johnny.

He looked at Tom.

Tom was asleep.

Johnny felt, and heard, the sled begin to groan and move. He watched the dogs, Rock at the front, climb the slope. He held on as the sled climbed behind them. He felt the sled speed up when they got to the top. He felt the wind on his face. He watched the dogs. He wanted to shout. *Wilderness!* He wanted to shout it. But he didn't. He didn't want to wake Tom.

The Airport

The plane had landed – it was up on the screen: LANDED – but her father still looked worried. Gráinne wanted to say something. She felt sorry for him, and embarrassed. There was a ketchup stain on his jumper and a bit of hardened shaving foam on the lobe of one of his ears. He watched the people coming through the arrivals gate. He moved again, and Gráinne had to follow him. Two boys walked through, but they weren't Tom and Johnny.

"What's keeping them?" he said.

"Do you want a cup of coffee or something?" said Gráinne.

"What?"

He shouted it. Then he smiled.

"Sorry," he said. "Did you say something about coffee?"

"Yes."

"No," he said. "I'd better not."

He looked at the arrivals gate again, and so did Gráinne – and they were there. Johnny and Tom. They were looking at the waiting faces.

Gráinne laughed.

She was surprised. She'd wanted to see them, but she hadn't expected it to fill her like this. She watched her father rush at them. They disappeared behind him – Gráinne couldn't see them for a second. Then she could, because her father was on his knees with his arms around them, and she could see them both talking before she could hear them, telling him about the holiday, and the snow, and the accident.

And then she saw her stepmother. Gráinne didn't know her at first, the woman in the wheelchair, in the big bubble jacket. Then it made sense, and she saw it was her stepmother. She watched her father stand up and walk to her stepmother, and he bent down, and they hugged. The crowds of people coming out had to go around them. There was a woman there who'd been pushing the wheelchair; and she stood, and waited, and looked a bit embarrassed. Then her father straightened up. He said something to the woman who'd been pushing the wheelchair. She shook hands with Gráinne's stepmother, and her father started pushing.

Gráinne waited.

Her brothers had seen her, and they were charging at her. Tom was holding something out. He stopped right in front of her and pushed it into her stomach.

"Here."

"What is it?" said Gráinne.

"Your present," said Tom. "It's cool."

"Hi, by the way," said Gráinne.

"Yeah, hi."

It was a small toy dog, wearing a T-shirt with "Where's The Beach?" on it.

"It's a husky," said Tom.

"Cool."

"It didn't cost that much," said Tom.

"Fine," said Gráinne.

She looked at Johnny.

"Hi."

"Hi."

"Good time?"

"Yeah, cool."

"Mam broke her leg in two places," said Tom.

"I know," said Gráinne.

"Two places," said Tom. "And I burned my thumb. See?'

Her stepmother was looking at her. She smiled. She looked tired.

"Hi, Gráinne," she said.

"Hi," said Gráinne.

"Thanks for coming," said her stepmother – Sandra. "It's lovely to see you."

Gráinne shrugged. She nodded at the leg, the way it was stretched out stiff in front of Sandra.

"Is it sore?" she said.

"No," said Sandra. "Actually, yeah. It's bloody killing me."

But she smiled. And Gráinne smiled. She tried to keep looking at Sandra.

"Hey, Gráinne. Guess what?"

It was Tom.

"What?"

"We're getting a husky."

Gráinne held out her toy dog.

"Like this?"

"Yeah, but real."

Gráinne said nothing.

"Real, Gráinne," said Tom. "We're getting a real one. For Christmas."

Gráinne spoke.

"Big deal," she said.

And she heard her father laughing.